"Do you know anything about vampires, the chiang-shih as the Chinese call them?"

"What? Are you going to tell me another story?"

"Bloody hell, just answer the question."

"Of course I know what a chiang-shih is. I had slumber parties, but I outgrew believing in them when I turned twelve."

"Enlighten me."

She took an exasperated breath. "The Chinese believe that a person has two souls. One soul can leave the body and roam the earth."

"Go on."

"If the two souls aren't reunited the body dies and the soul will roam the earth forgetting the human aspects, turning toward a more animalistic way of life, craving the essence of the living."

"Blood, the essence of life."

"Sure. Whatever." Her shoulder lifted in a shrug. "What does this have to do with my uncle or me for that matter?"

His gaze lingered over her. She squirmed but didn't look away. "Everything. I'm afraid you're in danger now. I've tasted you."

"Excuse me."

"The kiss."

"One kiss doesn't—"

"I know how your heart beats." He placed

his hand on his chest, tapping. "Thump-thump—thump-thump. I'm a vampire, a chiang-shih and I have two days to reunite my souls."

She stared at him for a blink of second before she turned and headed for the front door while mumbling under her breath. "You are a lunatic. Too bad, too, because you're a good-looking guy, not to mention a great kisser, but having a screw loose is where I draw the line. I've listened to what you had to say. Now I think you better leave."

He moved fast, faster than a human. He stood, leaning against the front door as if he'd been standing there all along.

She stopped in her tracks, turned around to make sure her eyes hadn't deceived her and that he truly had materialized in front of the door. He knew his movements would spook her, but he didn't have time for delicacy. He needed her to believe him.

"Holy, holy—how did you do that?" She looked at him again. "Are you some kind of magician?"

"I told you—vampire."

She backed up a step. "Okay, say you are. The chiang-shih of legend is known to have a hideous green phosphorescent glow about it, serrated teeth and long talons. You don't have any of that. Where are your fangs? Huh?" She whirled around to flee, but he was there in front of her, blocking her way.

She opened her mouth to scream but he was

quicker. He kissed her—again. He was a vampire and most of the time he craved blood, but with her he craved her mouth—among other things. He plundered, taking and damn if the woman didn't respond. She may be afraid of him but there was a connection between them, something that bonded them. She had to be the answer to his prayers.

Praises for Autumn Moon

"Autumn Moon" starts with action and doesn't stop. The romance is perfectly entwined with myth and suspense. A one night read."
~**Reviewed by Shona, Bitten By Books**~

"If you have a craving for a good vampire story, you don't want to miss out on 'Autumn Moon.' Read through the pages of this delightful 'love' story, as this unlikely pair attempt to conquer Jairec's curse before his time runs out, leading them into a sinful interlude."
~**Reviewed by Deanna, Ghost Writers Literary Review**~

"Ancient Chinese Vampires"
"Autumn Moon is a completely new take on the vampire genre, or rather I should say it's an ancient Asian version retold in a refreshing new light. Autumn Moon is one of those stories that comes at you unexpectedly and takes the vampire legend to an entirely different level."
~**Reviewed by Clover Autrey, PNR Romance Reviews**~

This is a very fast-paced piece, but it keeps the reader in the midst of the action. Ms. Nutt does a wonderful job of weaving a legend into the heart this romance.
~**Reviewed by Kimberly, Coffee Time Romance & More**~

"This books is great. I had a blast. We have an ancient evil, a tormented family, a hunky hero and his lovely lady, and plucky grandparents that are not afraid to kick some paranormal arse. Lovely work!"

~Brenda Thatcher, Co-Owner Mystique Books~

Autumn Moon
Karen Michelle Nutt

A vampire tale

An Otherworldly Tale
Presented by Twin Star Books
Autumn Moon
A vampire tale

ISBN-13: 978-0-578-05931-0
ISBN-10: 0-5780-5931-2

First Printing 2010 in the United States of America

Dedicated to Jairec Baker, the little boy with a very cool name.

Soul mate

"A man is a bird with one wing and he searches for his mate, the other wing."
~Chinese Proverb

Chapter One

San Francisco, California is known for its mild temperatures all year round and for its blessed fog during the summer months. In the morning, the mist acted as a magic cloak protecting Jairec Connelly, but now the enchantment wore off leaving the sun's rays sizzling the pavement like laser beams. Jairec pulled the hood of his sweatshirt down over his head, shading as much skin as deemed possible. Even with this effort, he could feel his skin burn. It wouldn't do if he burst into flames especially since he needed to keep a low profile.

From across the street, Jairec set up his stake out, watching the comings and goings of people entering *Moon's Acupuncture*, but still no sign of the man who could help him. He pursed his lips together. Help him? He'd have to convince him not to kill him first.

At 9:30, a woman with long dark hair dressed in a black suit and comfortable shoes opened the acupuncture shop, unlocking the doors from the inside. He glanced at the two windows above the shop. She must live in the apartment above like so many others did. Two other employees, one male, one female arrived a half an hour later, both in their early twenties. All three were of Asian descent, not surprising since this was Chinatown and the businesses were probably family owned. By noon, there was still no sign of Dr. Jin Lei.

Dr. Lei had what Jairec needed. He was willing to pay for his services, but if the good doctor wouldn't help him, he'd take it by force. He wasn't a violent man by nature, but this was a matter of life and death, his to be exact.

He'd wanted no part in this supernatural bullshit, but his wanker of a brother had dragged him into it anyway. Now Tristan was missing, and he had been turned into the undead. "Some holiday," he grumbled. He did what any preternatural freak would do. He listened. He waited and learned whom he needed to see. The other freaks—shapeshifters, demons, any who slinked out of their hidey-holes at night called her, "The Seer." She turned out to be a crotchety old woman named Gladys Seymour, living in the suburbs of downtown San Francisco. He thought back to what Gladys told him, wanting to make sure he didn't miss something.

***

Gladys allowed Jairec to enter her house and follow her to the kitchen. She wore a blue shift, sandals and her gray hair pulled back in a bun. The effects of his new life were taking its toll. He could hear her heart beating— bum-bump, bum-bump like a beacon calling him. He could smell the coppery tang of her blood flowing through her veins. The delicate skin at the base of her neck would prove no protection once he sunk his teeth into the flesh. He licked his lips in anticipation.

Her gaze snapped to his. "You take a bite out of me big boy and I'll—"

Against his will, his new acquired instincts took over and he lunged. She waved her hand, propelling him back with a magic blast from her fingertips. He slammed into the wall and slid to the floor. If he'd been human, she'd have killed him or at the very least rendered him unconscious. There were some perks to being one of the undead. He could take a beating and keep on ticking.

She pointed a finger at him, and he cringed, expecting another blast from her. "I'll forgive you this one slight because you're newly made. Make a second attempt, chiang-shih and you're toast. Do you got it?" Her dark eyes narrowed, warning him to behave. She stood maybe five-two, but the power radiating from her convinced him she meant every word.

"I apologize." He leaned against the wall for support as he came to his feet.

She nodded. She walked over to her refrigerator and took out a bottle containing a dark reddish liquid too thick to be red wine. He had a sickening feeling of what it was and recoiled when she jabbed it at him.

"Don't be a fool. If you don't drink it, you'll kill someone, and all will be lost then. Keeping a pure soul will be your salvation."

He took the bottle from her. He closed his eyes as he took a swig and hated that he liked the taste.

"Pig's blood," she answered his unasked question.

He drank every last drop, wiping his mouth with the back of his sleeve.

"Now sit." She pointed to the table. She went to her cabinet, took out a wooden bowl and filled it with water. She mumbled a chant or prayer of some sort before she gazed at the liquid.

He saw tap water.

The Seer obviously witnessed something else. "You will find the cure in Chinatown. Dr. Jin Lei's place."

"This doctor will know how to help me? He'll be able to turn me back to the way I was?"

"I only know the elixir of life will be found there." She hummed and weaved back and forth as if receiving some kind of psychic advice from the other side. "Autumn moon is your destiny. You must accept the elixir before the festival's end. If you do not, you'll remain cursed and walk among the undead for all eternity."

"Dr. Lei will hand over the cure. Just like that."

Her dark eyes riveted to him. "I never said it would be easy. He will most likely want to kill you."

"I'm already dead, a vampire. Or what did you call me—a chiang-shih?"

She chuckled with no mirth. "I do hate the newly dead," she mumbled. "No moron. He will perform a ritual, sending your sorry ass to hell." She rose from her seat and walked over to her bookcase. She moved books aside and shuffled through the magazines, finally pulling an issue out. She opened it up and ripped out a page. "Here," she said handing it to him. "This is a picture of Dr. Lei. A few years ago a magazine did an article about his herbal remedies."

***

Two days ago, Jairec would have laughed at The Seer's eerie premonition and her ill-gotten advice. Now he was living proof that creatures of the night existed, walking among the living in wait of an opportunity to strike.

Chinatown held an annual Autumn Moon Festival, which so happened to be this weekend. If he went by what The Seer told him, this gave him three days to convince Dr. Lei to help him. He would use any means he could. He wouldn't succumb to his fate so readily.

When Dr. Lei never showed up to work, he began to give up hope. He jogged across the street. Since his unnatural demise, his hearing had improved, so much so that he had the urge to put earplugs in his ears. Today it would come in handy to eavesdrop and hopefully find out when the employees expected Dr. Lei.

"Don't forget to deliver the package your grandmother left you," the young female employee told the woman who had opened the shop. "She said it's a matter of life and death."

The woman who opened the shop shook her head. "Yes, of course it is."

Her voice was smooth, silky like a caress. She wore her straight, black hair pulled back in a ponytail, letting the long strands cascade down her back. She looked worried as she chewed on her lower lip. Then she sighed. "I might as well take care of the delivery now. Get it off my hands before it's too late."

Jairec smiled. This could be it. Maybe he wouldn't need Dr. Lei after all. He turned away as the woman left the shop. *Life and death, a need to get it off her hands*—he'd follow her and see where she led him. Maybe he should just steal the package. One small woman wouldn't be a challenge to subdue.

Chapter Two

Autumn headed for Sying's Tea Shop. The package her grandmother entrusted to her was in the white bag she carried. Chinatown buzzed with activity as the shop owners prepared for the annual Autumn Moon Festival, the festival she'd been named for since she'd been born during the festivities twenty-four years ago. She smiled with anticipation for what the weekend would bring.

She looked forward to hearing The Tamaka Golden Sun Chinese Opera Group play. They were scheduled to perform on Saturday at the Commercial Alley stage. Grant Ave. held another stage and would host Chinese Music throughout the day. Vendors lined the streets for the tourists to sample authentic Chinese food and bubble tea drinks, while they enjoyed the dances, parades and the dim sum demonstrations. With all the small family owned businesses, Chinatown relied on tourism to make ends meet. The Autumn Moon Festival drew in large crowds. She would

15

have her own booth where she offered her art of acupuncture. For a small fee, the tourists would be amazed how quickly a few well-placed needles would soothe their tired feet. Her grandparents had set up a booth, too.

They ran *Sinfully Sweet Bakery*, known for their custard-filled creations and sugary lotus seed moon cakes. They had a booth not far from where hers was set up. Autumn learned how to bake at her grandmother's side while being immersed into the Chinese world of history and tradition. She loved her grandparents but missed her parents.

Her mother, Lillian Lei hated the strict rules of her life. She'd wanted more than to work day in and day out in Chinatown. She ran away from home at seventeen and married Quinn Moon, a singer in a mediocre band visiting from Ireland. Nine months later, Autumn had been born. She inherited her mother's straight black hair, and her father's Irish green eyes. For all her mother's rashness, she and her father had been happy for the seven years they were married. They stayed a family, traveling where her father's band played. They were never apart. Except for that night, the night her parents were taken from her.

Autumn had a bad cold and her parents left her with a babysitter. A car accident took them away and Autumn came to live with her mother's parents since her father's family was long gone.

In those first horrible years without them,

Autumn used to pretend her father was one of the immortals and he'd been summoned back to the heavens and her mother had followed him there. Autumn knew it was a silly story, but as a child it made her feel better believing her parents were still alive and looking after her.

Autumn crossed the street, avoiding the trolley that was probably on its way to one of the other scenic neighborhoods of San Francisco.

She headed down the alleyway, planning to enter through the back door of the teashop. She raised her hand to knock, but someone grabbed her from behind and slammed her into the wall, knocking the wind out of her. Her attacker locked the thickness of his arm against her neck while his muscular body leaned against her, pinning her against the hard stone.

"Give me the package and we won't have any problems."

Autumn's eyes widened as she stared into two sea-smoked colored eyes. She lifted the package that she was to deliver to Mr. Sying.

He yanked it out of her hand. "Now don't follow me or I'll be forced to do something you'll regret."

Autumn could only manage to nod her head.

"Hey, are you okay down there?" someone yelled from the street, probably a tourist since she didn't recognize him. He was tall and blond definitely not from Chinatown.

It was nice to know that there were people who'd stop to help. Before she could choke out her plea, the man holding her hostage covered her mouth with his lips. She should have stopped him, bit him, did something other than let the bastard kiss her. Man, could he kiss, ravishing her lips, teeth and tongue as unapologetic as it was seductive. Logic fled and she moaned into his mouth stunned by the force, the need to have more. She kissed him back.

When he released her, they stared into each other's heavily lidded eyes. The air shimmered around them taunt, waiting to pull them under again. The intensity of the immediate attraction mystified her and yet she felt as if she'd been waiting for him all her life. Obviously, the sensation, the connection hadn't gone unnoticed by him. He raked his fingers through his hair; uncertainty lit his eyes as his gaze held hers. She teetered on her feet ready to step toward him, but she drew in a rugged breath and sanity slapped her in the face. She didn't know what crazy notion had come over her, but whatever it was, she had no intentions of repeating it. She glanced to see if her would-be-rescuer was still at the end of the alleyway. No such luck. The guy obviously thought they were lovers, sneaking away for a late afternoon tryst.

Her attacker backed away from her further. She thought he'd say something. Threaten her more or kiss her. She'd much rather he'd kiss her. She shook her head. What in the world was she thinking? She should scream, but before she could react, he turned on his heels, fled down the shadowed alleyway and disappeared around the corner.

Autumn stood there wondering what had just happened, but what mystified her even more was why had the stranger been so bent on stealing her grandmother's moon cakes?

Chapter Three

Jairec kept his hood down over his head, keeping his pace so not to be caught. He expected the woman to yell for help, but she didn't. He could feel her heated gaze watching him as he made his escape. He held on tight to the package. It was his salvation. The Seer said Dr. Jin Lei kept the cure at Moon's Acupuncture, but it would not be given easily. Once he heard the women talk about the package, he knew it had to be important. "Life or death, she said." He tried convincing himself he had no other choice than to steal the package, but did he need to kiss the woman?

He hadn't meant to, but when the pedestrian asked if she was okay, he knew she'd scream and kissing her seemed the best course of action at the time. He didn't expect the jolt the kiss gave him. He thought her attractive with her slim figure, jet-black hair and unusual forest green eyes, but the kiss sparked something in him he'd not felt in a long time.

"Forget it Connelly, you don't need that kind of distraction right now." If he was going to pull through this, he had to stay focused. Besides, if she knew his diet consisted of pig's blood, while he fought off the desire to suck the blood from the nearest human ... He shook his head. Yeah, it would be a sure turn off.

He opened the door to his hotel room and locked it behind him. He tore open the bag and lifted the lid to the white box. He stared at the pastry for half a second. "This is the cure?"

He shrugged. Who was he to argue? He grabbed the pastry and shoved it into his mouth. Normally, he loved sweets, but since he'd been cursed all earthly food made him gag. This was no different, but he forced it down anyway.

He stood waiting for something to happen, some kind of miraculous transformation. Then he felt something, a churning in his stomach. He felt sweaty, shaky and ... "Shit!" He ran to the bathroom. Grabbing the sides of the toilet, he threw up.

This wasn't the cure.

He flushed the toilet and grabbed one the towels on the rack to wipe his face. He went back into the room and picked up the box with the sweets. "Sinfully Sweet Bakery." He read off the label. The woman hadn't been sneaking out Jin's secret cure for the undead. She'd been delivering bakery goods. She tricked him, but he wouldn't let her get away with it.

Chapter Four

With her latte in one hand, Autumn unlocked the door to Moon's Acupuncture, the shop she took over from her Great Uncle Jin. Jin Lei, her grandfather's brother never had children and he treated Autumn like a daughter, teaching her the ancient Chinese rituals to go along with her school training when she became a licensed practitioner.

Jin's naming the shop Moon's Acupuncture after her last name was purely a coincidence.

Autumn's grandmother insisted there was no such thing as a coincidence. Jin must have foreseen Autumn's roll in running the shop after he no longer could. Perhaps, but then maybe her uncle just had a thing for the moon. She looked around her shop at her uncle's chosen artwork. Photos of the moon phases, prints of the full moon, and oils depicting the moon as the main focus. Her grandmother also believed Autumn had contracted a cold, so she'd be spared from her parents' fate. Autumn didn't buy into the superstitious nonsense.

Autumn placed her purse behind the counter where her glass jars of herbs decorated the long wall. The phone rang and she picked it up, leaning against the counter. "Hello Grandmother. Yes, yes, I'm fine. Yes, I stopped at the coffee shop this morning and no one accosted me." Autumn wished she could have kept her strange encounter with the moon-cake-thief to herself, but she'd been left with no choice since she had to tell Mr. Sying why she didn't have the package. Of course, she left out the part about the mind-shattering kiss. "I guess the guy only liked your pastries." She chuckled then cleared her throat. "Sorry Grandmother, I know, I know. That wasn't funny. Don't worry. I'm fine. I need to gather a few things for my booth, and I'll be locking up. I love you, too." She hung up the phone.

"Close family."

Autumn jumped at the sound of the man's voice. She knew it was him even before she turned around, but seeing the tall brooding man with hair, thick like the devil's dark velvet still made her heart skip a beat. "How did you get in here?"

"I have my ways." He gave her a careless shrug.

He had a slight accent, betraying his Irish heritage. She missed that yesterday, but he'd been more intent on shoving his tongue down her throat than talking. "Working on a criminal record, are we?" She backed away, feeling beneath the counter for the button that would summon the police.

"Don't do it."

She froze. "What?"

"Call the police. Hear me out and then I'll

leave."

"Okay," she said carefully.

He grinned, but the smile didn't quite meet his eyes. "I just want the package."

"You took the moon cakes yesterday. If you want more, you'll have to buy them like everyone else—at the bakery."

"You know that isn't what I mean. You're a real corker, lady. I bet you had a real good laugh."

"Frankly mister I don't find any of this humorous. I have no idea what you're after, but it's obvious you have the wrong person."

"Perhaps you're right. I need to speak to Dr. Jin Lei. Do you know where I can find him?"

"My uncle?" She lifted her brows.

"He owns this place, doesn't he?"

"He did. He passed away. What exactly are looking for? Maybe I can help." The man was obviously a lunatic. The full moon brought out the worst and they were still two days shy of the full moon.

"He's dead?" The look on his face changed to disbelief then shock over the discovery. If Autumn didn't know better, she'd think he was frightened. He ran his hand through his hair. "That can't be right. She said, Chinatown. She was insistent that I come here."

"Who told you to come here?"

His gaze locked onto hers. "She told me I would find the elixir of life. I assumed the acupuncturist, your uncle would have it here.

It made sense. Look at the herbs you have and concoctions of every sort." He waved his hand around the room, indicating the shelves lined with bottles.

"Did you say the elixir of life?"

"Aye. Do you know how to make it?"

"You aren't serious?" Her lips twitched and a husky laugh of amusement escaped. "You do realize the story is a Chinese legend. It isn't real."

***

Jairec pinned her down with his gaze. "All legends have a bit of the truth to them."

"Is that so?"

He heard the humor in her voice and knew she only patronized him, but he had to make her believe him. Time was running out for him. Such a pretty woman with long dark hair and forest green eyes, he'd be loathed to find out he'd killed her once the change was completed. "Your uncle must have told you about the cure."

"He instructed me on many cures but none that would give a person eternal life. That's mad."

"I don't want eternal life. Trust me, it isn't what it's cracked up to be. I want my life back. Two days ago, I might have agreed with you that what I ask is crazy, but now I believe anything is possible. I have to because my life depends on it."

"Okay." She drew out the word, eyeing him

warily.

He knew she didn't believe him. He wouldn't in her place, but he had to convince her. "Do you know anything about vampires, the chiang-shih as the Chinese call them?"

"What? Are you going to tell me another story?"

"Bloody hell, just answer the question."

"Of course I know what a chiang-shih is. I had slumber parties, but I outgrew believing in them when I turned twelve."

"Enlighten me."

She took an exasperated breath. "The Chinese believe that a person has two souls. One soul can leave the body and roam the earth."

"Go on."

"If the two souls aren't reunited the body dies and the soul will roam the earth forgetting the human aspects, turning toward a more animalistic way of life, craving the essence of the living."

"Blood, the essence of life."

"Sure. Whatever." Her shoulder lifted in a shrug. "What does this have to do with my uncle or me for that matter?"

His gaze lingered over her. She squirmed but didn't look away. "Everything. I'm afraid you're in danger now. I've tasted you."

"Excuse me."

"The kiss."

"One kiss doesn't—"

"I know how your heart beats." He placed

his hand on his chest, tapping. "Thump-thump—thump-thump. I'm a vampire, a chiang-shih and I have two days to reunite my souls."

She stared at him for a blink of second before she turned and headed for the front door while mumbling under her breath. "You are a lunatic. Too bad, too, because you're a good-looking guy, not to mention a great kisser, but having a screw loose is where I draw the line. I've listened to what you had to say. Now I think you better leave."

He moved fast, faster than a human. He stood, leaning against the front door as if he'd been standing there all along.

She stopped in her tracks, turned around to make sure her eyes hadn't deceived her and that he truly had materialized in front of the door. He knew his movements would spook her, but he didn't have time for delicacy. He needed her to believe him.

"Holy, holy—how did you do that?" She looked at him again. "Are you some kind of magician?"

"I told you—vampire."

She backed up a step. "Okay, say you are. The chiang-shih of legend is known to have a hideous green phosphorescent glow about it, serrated teeth and long talons. You don't have any of that. Where are your fangs? Huh?" She whirled around to flee, but he was there in front of her, blocking her way.

She opened her mouth to scream but he was

quicker. He kissed her—again. He was a vampire and most of the time he craved blood, but with her he craved her mouth—among other things. He plundered, taking and damn if the woman didn't respond. She may be afraid of him but there was a connection between them, something that bonded them. She had to be the answer to his prayers. He lifted his head. "Please don't be afraid of me, lass. I don't want to harm you. Don't scream and I'll prove to you I'm not lying."

She nodded. Her eyes still wide with fear or passion. He wasn't sure which.

He opened his mouth, baring his two canines that were longer and pointier than the other teeth.

Holy, holy—" Her gaze riveted to his. "You're telling me the truth."

"Aye and I need your help." He released her, sensing she wouldn't run.

"Listen, Fang Boy, not that I don't sympathize with your plight, but I don't know what I could do to help."

"There must be a cure, a mixture that will reverse this before I ..." He swallowed hard. "Lose my humanity. It's already difficult."

"What? Do you want to suck people's blood? Do you want mine?"

He looked at her and he knew he couldn't hide the wicked gleam in his eyes.

"Oh my God, you do." Her hand flew to her neck.

"I hear heart beats drumming in my head,

calling me. I hear yours, but I also want you. I feel this inner hunger, this need to touch you." He ran his hand through his hair in frustration. "I'm horny as hell. I don't know if I want to take your blood or make love to you."

"Horny? Yeah, I kinda got that.'

She glanced down at the bulge in his pants and if vampires could blush, he was sure he'd turned a nice shade of red.

"It seems some of the legend of chiang-shih still runs true," she commented, making him wonder what she meant. "I'm glad you still have some human control, Fang Boy. Are you able to cross water?"

He didn't have the chance to answer. The bell chimed on her door and a man walked in.

"Get rid of him," he warned.

"Don't threaten me, Fang-boy. Besides, I can't. It's Yi. He'll be suspicious if I usher him out the door."

Jairec wanted to know who Yi was to her. Someone close by the way the bastard let his gaze slide up and down her as if she were a tasty morsel. A low growl vibrated in the back of his throat. It shocked him and he covered his mouth with a cough. She frowned at him. Her expression clearly stating he'd better behave.

"We're not through here," Autumn hissed as she turned toward the door with a smile. "Yi, what brings you here this morning?"

Yi was twenty-something and stood nearly six feet tall with dark hair. His dark eyes pierced right through a person.

Jairec lifted his chin and stared back.

"Who's he?" Yi shrugged his head at Jairec.

"Oh ... that's uh ... Mr. Fang."

Jairec's lips twitched, but he managed not to smile.

He doesn't look Chinese."

"I don't look Irish, but my father was, so that makes me half," Autumn countered back.

So she was Irish as well. That would account for the green eyes, Jairec thought.

Yi harrumphed. "Your grandmother asked me to check on you."

"I told her I was fine."

"She said you had some trouble yesterday." Yi eyed Jairec with suspicion.

"It was probably some homeless guy and he smelled Grandmother's moon cakes. No harm."

"Hmmm. Still I'll walk with you."

"Sure. Let me get my things." She nervously looked at Yi then Jairec.

Jairec let her off the hook. "I'll be by later for—my session."

She nodded. "Good. Stay out of trouble, Mr. Fang."

He approached her and took her hand. "Please call me Jairec."

She smiled. "Jairec."

"May I call you ..."

"Autumn," she told him.

"Dr. Moon to you," Yi chimed in obviously not liking how close they stood.

"Autumn Moon," Jairec rolled the name off his tongue, realizing the significance of what it meant. "You're the one."

"Excuse me?"

"Until later." He kissed the top of her hand then headed for the front door. He felt Yi's gaze follow him out. Yi had the right not to trust him, but he disliked the guy all the same.

He pulled the sweatshirt's hood over his head, wondering as he did so how long it would be before he wouldn't be able to tolerate the sun.

Chapter Five

"I swear I met Mr. Fang somewhere before—if Fang is even his name. I don't like him," Yi told her as he watched Jairec cross the street.

"You don't know him."

"Neither do you." He looked at her, his eyes narrowing. "Do you?"

"Don't worry so much Yi." She rolled her eyes. "Mr. Fang is a client. You do realize I see patients here."

"Hmm, yes I know, but I do worry all the same. You're a beautiful woman, Autumn and men will want to take advantage of you."

"If a problem arises, I'll handle the situation." She turned away, but he reached for her, gripping her shoulders so she'd look at him.

"You know how I feel about you."

She did know, but she didn't feel the same way about him. He wanted a submissive Chinese woman who looked pretty by his side and didn't speak her mind. She didn't fit the mold, never had, but Yi refused to see it. "Yi let's not go there, okay."

He let his hands fall away to his side. "I can take care of you."

"I'm perfectly able to take care of myself."

He harrumphed. "I want to marry you, Autumn. Our families would be happy with the match."

"No doubt," she mumbled as she turned away.

"What did you say?"

"I'm not ready for marriage."

"When will you be?"

If anything, Yi was persistent. She met his gaze, his eyes betraying his feelings for her. Why couldn't he understand, she didn't want to marry him. They didn't belong together. "I don't know. Maybe never. You shouldn't wait for me, Yi. You need to find someone else who will appreciate you."

Yi took her bag from her. "Can I help it that I set my eyes on you?" He kissed the top of her head. "I can wait for you to be ready."

"Yi—"

"Shush." He placed a finger on her lips, silencing her words. "You say you don't want to marry me."

She nodded her head.

"I'll have to change your mind then, won't I?"

Chapter Six

Satisfied that Autumn was safely delivered at her grandparent's bakery, Yi left to open his antique shop. He promised to stop by later. She hoped he wouldn't.

The bell overhead rang as Autumn stepped over the threshold. Her grandmother, Mei Lei was four-foot eleven and slim. She'd turned sixty-seven on her last birthday and her hair was still dark as night with only a few gray strands peeking through her bun. She wore a long traditional gown with a floral print for the weekend's festivities. Autumn stuck to her jeans, but her sleeveless blouse had a Mandarin collar, giving it an oriental flair. Lilies and roses of fuchsia and periwinkle adorned the cream-colored blouse and there was a drawstring on the left side, raising it high on her slim hip.

"Autumn, I thought you were heading over to the booth."

"I can head over there later. Loann and Bruce should be there now. I thought you might need some help."

"I do. The parade starts at eleven and I need

to have the pastries at the booth soon or we won't be able to get by the crowds."

"Does Grandfather have the truck out back?"

"Yes. I also made some fortune cookies, too. I don't know why tourists demand to have them as if they're some great Chinese delicacy. The Chinese didn't even know what they were until Golden Gate Fortune Cookies opened their doors in 1962. If they want tradition, we could put little idiotic notes in the moon cakes as the Chinese patriots did to fool the Mongolian rulers. Now that would be authentic."

Autumn smiled as she followed her grandmother to the kitchen. She liked to grumble. Grandfather insisted this was what kept her young.

"Grandmother, may I ask you something?"

"So serious. What is it Autumn?"

She felt silly asking, but she needed information fast and she knew her grandmother believed in the legends. "What do you know about the chiang-shih?"

Her grandmother whirled around so fast that Autumn had to take a step back. "Shush. Don't say the name in my store. It will bring bad luck to all of us."

"What do you know of it?"

"The being is evil and must be cast back to hell."

"Always? It's always evil."

Her grandmother's eyes narrowed. What is this talk about Autumn? Are you in danger?"

"No, of course not. I was interested in the legend."

"All legends have a bit of truth to it."

That was what Jairec had told her.

"It's best not to bring them up. Words are like incantations and once spoken to the winds you can't take them back."

Her grandmother was superstitious, but then she'd lived more years than Autumn had. Who's to say she didn't know what she spoke of? Autumn cleared her throat. "How would you rid yourself of it?"

"Child what has happened? Does this have something to do with the man who stole my moon cakes?"

Autumn chuckled. "What would a chiang—one of the undead want with moon cakes? Aren't they only after blood?"

"Hmmm. They're after your soul. They can look like monsters if their human counterpart had been evil, but if they were cursed or suffered a violent death, they may look pleasant to the eye. Do not be fooled by a pretty face, Autumn."

She wouldn't call Jairec's face beautiful but more rugged, weathered in a sexy-all-I-want-to-do-is-kiss-you kind of look. "They're always dangerous?"

"They're evil."

"Only if they've killed." The deep voice rumbled from behind them.

Autumn and her grandmother, both turned at the same time to find Chin standing in the archway.

"Hello, grandfather," Autumn greeted him. "So, they aren't always evil."

He stared at her with suspicion, his eyes narrowing, but then he answered her. "Only if the fiend has killed to quench its thirst is it evil. It must make the first kill, an innocent. It must suck the life force from its victim to live."

"And if they haven't done this?" Autumn pushed, needing to know the answer.

He walked over to her, his gaze locking onto hers as he spoke. "There is still a chance to redeem them."

Autumn knew her grandparents were worried. Her grandmother was mumbling the prayer of protection and her grandfather's expression showed fear that she'd come in contact with one of the undead. God, they really believed the legend was real. What was she thinking? She'd met the legend and he kissed like the Irish devil he was.

Chin placed his hand on her arm. "You must be careful, Autumn. They can be persuasive, seducers not only of the mind but of the body."

She already knew that. "Don't worry, Grandfather. It's not like the ... you know the undead are walking among us." She chuckled and didn't quite meet his gaze. "I was only curious." She shrugged and lifted one of the trays ready for the festival. "Should I load this in the truck?"

Chapter Seven

Jairec thought back to the night he was made, if this was the correct term to use. He remembered walking down to the wharf waiting for his brother to show.

"Meet me at Castagnolia's," Tristan had told him. *"We'll get a few drinks and have a bite to eat."*

He suspected Tristan was involved with something underhanded. He didn't know what, but trouble and Tristan went hand in hand. He looked over his brother's shoulder at the white-haired man dressed in ancient oriental garb. He paced back and forth in the shadows. Jairec didn't like him. He gave him the heebie-jeebies. "How about we get that drink now, Tristan?" Jairec met his brother's gaze. Tristan's eyes were the same shade of sea-smoke gray as his were, but Tristan's hair was light brown like their mother's.

Tristan hesitated as if he'd like to take him up on it, but then he glanced behind him at the white-haired man and shook his head. "I have business to take care of, but after..." He met his gaze once more. "After I'm done, I'll be free."

That was the last time he'd seen his brother. When he didn't show, Jairec went looking for him. He thought he spotted Tristan. He called to him, but he disappeared around the corner of a building, bringing him closer to the wharf. The pungent smell of fish and garbage hit his nostrils, making him gag, but he didn't slow his pace. What a fool he'd been. He ignored the warning bells going off in his head that this was a bad idea. He rounded the bend, but no one was there or at least he had thought no one was there until someone slammed a lead bar into his skull.

He tried not to lose consciousness, but the world spun in and out. The white-haired man stood over him and he chanted in a singsong voice as he performed the perverse ritual. Jairec would swear he felt energy pulse through him as if the molecules of his body were changing. Then the white-haired bloke brought down the bar again and the rest was history. Now he was the living dead and that scared the hell out of him.

The Seer said to go to Jin Lei's shop in Chinatown. It's the moon festival, she told him. Autumn moon is your destiny. Not autumn moon the festival, but perhaps she meant Autumn Moon the person, the beautiful woman with forest green eyes. Even with him being dead, she could entice him to forget his mission. Under other circumstances, he would have asked Autumn out, but now he wouldn't dare. Dating a vampire would prove detrimental to her health.

Autumn Moon is your destiny. The Seer's words couldn't be just a coincidence. Autumn had to have the answer, but what? Some kind of concoction she would mix with herbs and bring him back to life? He doubted it. Maybe she was to help him move on to the next life. Damn, he wasn't ready to go. He had too much he wanted to do here. Number one on his list was to find the white-haired man and give him a taste of the Connelly hospitality. He wouldn't resort to underhanded backstabbing, but a straightforward punch in the nose would do. Then, he'd kill the bastard.

Chapter Eight

Autumn could see the opening parade from her booth. Her grandparents' table stood two booths over from her booth. The fog had finally burned off and the sun shone warm, making it a perfect day to be outdoors. Autumn smiled as the children marched into view wearing elaborate costumes. The band played the tunes they had practiced for the last few months.

"Ooh look there's George." Loann pointed.

Loann was dating George, He was one of the guys, who played the part of the lion. The lion dance dated back some thousand years, as far back as the Han Dynasties. The lion expressed joy and happiness. If Loann's smile was any indication, Autumn believed the dance worked like magic.

"They're good," Autumn agreed. "Since Bruce didn't show up, we'll close up about three. I want to see the martial artists. I hear they're better than the group who performed last year."

"Splendid. I can meet up with George then." Loann looked at Autumn. "I wonder what happened to Bruce. I tried his cell earlier, but no answer."

"We'll probably hear from him later." Autumn wasn't too worried. Bruce worked part time. He cared for his ailing grandfather and sometimes couldn't come in. She'd call later and make sure everything was all right.

The parade headed toward Washington Street where the main stage was set up. The first performers would be the Polynesian dancers.

For a moment, Autumn lost interest in the parade. A strange unease assaulted her as if someone watched her. The hairs on her arms stood up and goose flesh rippled up her back. She glanced at the street-filled tourists, snapping pictures and enjoying the morning as they sipped bubble tea drinks and snacked on pastries. No one looked suspicious. Then she spotted him. A white-haired man standing toward the back of the crowd, shaded from the sun. For a moment, she'd swear his eyes glowed red. His gaze held hers and his thin lips curved into an evil twist that sent a chill down her spine.

"Autumn, are you all right?"

She turned toward Loann. "Uh ... uh ... I'm fine." When she looked back toward the crowd, the white-haired man had vanished.

Maybe she'd only imagined him or perhaps it had only been a trick of the light. Of course, it made sense why she saw a boogieman. She just found out the chiang-shih of legends really existed. What other horrors lurked in the shadows? Not that Jairec would be what she'd imagined the chiang-shih to look like. His hair was too dark, his eyes were too gray, but he did send her libido up a notch. The chiang-shih was a sexual creature and Jairec had kissed her twice, leaving her wanting more. She sighed over the memory of the way his lips took hers.

"What are you thinking about?" Loann broke through her reverie.

"What?"

"You're wearing a silly grin. If I didn't know better, I'd say you're smitten with someone."

Smitten? More like the hots. She shook her head. What was she thinking? Jairec didn't have a pulse. She needed him to move on and leave her alone.

"Hello sweetheart, miss me?"

She whirled around to face the devil himself. Damn if her heart didn't race. "No, not really," she whispered back, hoping her voice didn't betray her.

Jairec frowned but didn't comment. He looked toward Loann who smiled up at him.

Autumn cleared her throat. "Loann, why don't you take a break?"

"I'm fine," she said all dreamy like as she gazed up at Jairec as if he were a god.

"Loann," she snapped.

"What?" She tore her gaze away from Jairec.

"Go over to my grandparents' booth. They have tea and moon cakes for you."

"Fine." She didn't seem happy to go, but she

did. She only glanced over her shoulder once before she lost interest.

"Do you have this effect on everyone?" Autumn accused.

"What effect?" His eyebrows furrowed.

He really didn't know. Autumn sighed and decided she wasn't going to enlighten him about his charming allure he had on women. He proved dangerous enough without him trying. "What do you want Jairec?"

"I need your help."

"I don't believe acupuncture will help you."

"I believe you have the elixir I seek whether you know it or not."

Autumn's attention was drawn to the parade as the actors imitating the immortal moon goddess, Chang O and the god, Hou Yi came into view. Their elaborate ceremonial garb was done in cream, red and gold. The legend stated the two knew of an elixir of life. They paid a hefty price for having it. The goddess was banished to the moon and the god became stranded on earth. Only once a year could the two come together. "Maybe you should talk to them." She pointed, jabbing her thumb at the performers. "They're the gods. The elixir of life is theirs to give."

"Do you think this is funny?"

"No, Fang Boy I don't."

"We're back to name calling again, I see."

"I need you gone. I have a business to run."

"I understand how it is. You can't be

bothered with a dead bloke. I get it."

He knew how to hit below the belt, making her feel guilty when she shouldn't. "If I knew how to help you, I would. Maybe you should let this life go. Move on." She waved her hand in front of her. "Don't you see a white light or something?"

"No. I'm cursed, Autumn. If I don't find the cure by the end of your Moon Festival, I'm damned to be a vampire, one that will kill your neighbors and friends. Do you really want their deaths on your hands?"

She chewed on her lower lip. "Why me? I don't know what I could do to help. I work with needles."

"Aye, and herbs."

She nodded. "To help the mind and soul, but I don't have a magical cure to bring you back to life. If I did, my schedule would be full for years."

"Maybe your Uncle Jin had the cure. Maybe something he put together. I don't know a secret formula of some sort."

"There isn't—" Then she did remember something. She looked up at Jairec. "This could be irrelevant, but My Uncle Jin had a book he used to jot down notes in. He said it was his recipe book."

He nodded his head. "That's good. This could be it."

She didn't want to give him false hope. "Slow down Fang Boy, I don't know what's in the book, but I'll pull it out and rifle through it."

"Thank you."

"Don't thank me yet. I frankly don't think I can help you."

"The Seer said you could."

"I thought you needed to see my Uncle Jin."

"She said Autumn Moon is my destiny." He met her startled gaze. "I had thought she meant the festival, but she never stated the festival as my destiny, only I must find the cure by the end of it."

Autumn chuckled. "How could I be your destiny? I don't know you."

He leaned close...too close. She would have backed away, but his hand gripped her arm, holding her in place. His eyelids closed in a slow deliberate blink as he inhaled. "Mmmm. Your scent is like an aphrodisiac. Surely you feel the pull as I do." He released her and met her gaze, pinning her down for an answer.

"I..." She swallowed the lump in the back of her throat. "I'm drawn to you, but so was Loann."

"Who?" His right brow rose in question.

"My assistant. The one I sent away because she couldn't keep her eyes off you."

His mouth slid into a smile. "Ah. You were jealous, hey?"

"I was no such thing." She inhaled deeply and brushed her hands over her shirt as if straightening it.

He chuckled. "It's okay. I didn't fancy leaving you with Yi this morning."

"With Yi? He's only friend." She waved her hand in dismissal.

"He wants more." There was no mistaking the low growl in his throat.

Her eyebrows lifted. "Now who sounds jealous?"

He rolled his beautiful eyes that spoke of honesty, not treachery of the chiang-shih.

"You haven't killed anyone." She meant it as a statement, but he answered anyway.

"No. I haven't. And I'd like to keep it that way."

She placed her hand on his arm. It was cool to the touch, but an electrical charge sifted through her, warming her from the inside out. A protective feeling she didn't care to dwell on set her actions in motion. She'd help him anyway she could. "I'll look through my uncle's books. We'll work to find the cure, but until then ... hmm... May I ask how you tame the blood lust?"

He looked embarrassed as he turned away not meeting her gaze. "Pig's blood."

"Good, let's keep it that way. Take a seat. I want to try something."

"Excuse me." He looked at her with suspicion.

She waved to the cushioned foldout chair. "I have an idea. I think it will help you."

He eyed her for a blink of second before he decided to trust her. He plopped himself down, stretching his long legs in front of him. She opened her pack that was on the table, exposing the needles she would need to use. Sitting down, Jairec was eye level with her, but she ignored his intent gaze. She needed a steady hand and his heated gaze made her nervous. She brushed away the wisps of hair on the side of head, exposing his ear.

He jerked away. "What are you doing?" He looked at her tools then her. "I'm not a voodoo doll. Don't think you're poking me with those."

She shook her head. "I'm trying to help. Now stop being a baby and sit still. It won't hurt." She forced herself not to smile. A big tough vamp and he was afraid of needles. "Well?"

He didn't exactly relax but he leaned his head to the side, exposing the ear. She placed two small needles behind the upper portion of the lobe. "Now that wasn't so bad."

"You're just going to leave them?"

"Yes. I don't know if it will work on a chiang-shih since I've never treated one, but on a human, it helps to curve the appetite for an addiction."

"You hope I won't crave blood."

"That's the point of this experiment."

He nodded and stood. "Let's hope it works."

"Meet me at the shop later tonight after the festivities die down. We'll take a look at my uncle's book." She turned away but he grabbed her hand.

"Thank you."

"I told you, don't thank me yet. We still have a long haul and in the end, I may still have to ..." She pursed her lips together, not wanting to voice what might have to be done, but it seemed he already knew.

"End my existence? Aye, I know." His gaze wavered over her as if memorizing her features. "I trust you, Autumn. No matter what you have to do, I know it will be the best decision." He leaned down and brushed his lips against her cheek before turning around and disappearing within the crowd.

The man could be so cryptic and sexy all in one—not bad for being dead.

Chapter Nine

Autumn arrived back at the shop a little after four. She put her supplies from the booth on the counter before she went upstairs to her apartment and put the bag she picked up at the butchers in the refrigerator. The day had been profitable with the streets crowded with tourists. Her booth was busy, but she kept checking her watch wishing the time would go by faster.

She headed for the bathroom to wash her face. She always felt refreshed when she did that. She needed a clear mind if she was going to weed through her uncle's notes. After she changed into a pair of jeans and her comfy *Bon Jovi* T-shirt, she headed back downstairs to the store and into the back room where her uncle liked to work. She hadn't the heart to clean it out after he died and now, she was glad she hadn't. The wood shelves were lined with jars filled with herbs. He kept the journal in the workbench's top drawer. It was locked, but she had keys. She hoped one of them opened the drawer.

"Did you find anything?"

Autumn jumped at the sound of his voice and the keys slipped from her grip, clattering to the floor. "Do you mind not sneaking up on a girl, Jairec?"

He bent down to retrieve the keys. He handed them to her. "Sorry. I guess I'm quiet on my feet."

"Yeah." She turned toward the drawer and tried the different keys, but none of them worked. "How'd you get in here anyway? I locked the doors."

"I have my ways."

She looked at him, her brows furrowing. "Supernatural?"

"It's a Boston special." His shoulders lifted in a shrug.

"Boston ...what?"

"My brother, Tristan showed me how to pick a lock. He pegged the name."

"Nice brother," she said sarcastically."

"Yeah. He was always getting into trouble."

"Is it just you and your brother then?"

"No. My mum lives in Ireland, Adara in County Donegal to be exact. She runs a shop selling the famed Donegal wool. My da is in Boston. My parents split up when Tristan and I were just little kids. Mum went back home with us, and Da stayed in the States. When Tristan turned fifteen my mum had enough of his shenanigans and felt I wasn't far behind in causing her grief. She shipped us to our da deciding we needed a firm hand. Tristan rebelled. He was in trouble more than not which didn't sit well with our da, who was the chief of police."

"I would say not. And you? Were you a troublemaker, too?"

"Not unless my brother dragged me into the foray of his mess." He shrugged.

"So you were a good boy—sometimes."

"You could say that I suppose."

She looked at him and he grinned.

"Right." She shook her head. She had a hunch he wasn't all that innocent. "So what did you do back in Boston?"

"I worked on website designs, creating and programming. It's a booming market right now."

"Oh, I can imagine. I want to set up a website. I didn't realize I could hire someone to put it together for me." She tried the last key with no luck. "Shoot, none of these work."

"Let me try."

She waved her hand to the drawer. "Be my guest."

In a few seconds, he had the drawer open.

"How did— never mind I don't need to know." She rummaged through the drawer, finding the journal shoved to the back. She took the book out and opened it. She glanced at the entries and frowned. "These are more like incantations than formulas." She flipped the page and stared at the drawing of a creature: longhaired, pointed canines and long clawed hands. "Now this is what the chiang-shih should look like. It would give a person a warning they're about to be attacked." She glanced up, her gaze sweeping over him. "You're too good-looking."

"Thank you, I think." He looked over her shoulder at the drawing. "The man or whatever he was who did this to me chanted something before he hit me over the head."

She looked at him. "Do you remember what he said?"

"No." He ran his hand through his hair. "I was disoriented. He seemed determined to beat my brains in, but then maybe he had second thoughts. I don't know."

"But to what purpose? Why would he want to turn you into the living dead? Then leave you to figure out your new life?"

"Do crazy people have to have a logical reason? Who knows maybe the bloke has a perverted mind and gets his jollies turning people into monsters."

"If he was one of the chiang-shih, they eventually kill. There haven't been any murders. I can't see how he could have kept that quiet."

"I have a theory. Tourists and the homeless—they disappear, and no one misses them for a while."

"Then it would mean he hadn't been doing this long. So where has he been hiding? You said you talk to the..."

"...Seer," he finished for her.

"Yes. Frankly, I don't understand why she sent you to me. What do I have to do with saving you?"

"I may be a vampire, but no one gave me a how-to-be-one book. Your uncle must have known the chiang-shih existed. Doesn't the journal prove that well enough?"

"I don't know what the journal proves." She looked at the book, her gaze landing on the hideous creature of legend. She swallowed back a lump in her throat. Would Jairec end up looking like this?

"Perhaps he knew of the chiang-shih, maybe other beings as well. He may have been keeping them at bay. You worked with him, didn't you?"

"Yes."

"Perhaps he showed you something that would help."

"He taught me a lot, but nothing comes to mind that would help you."

"I think you know more than you realize. Read the journal. Something will click. Something will prove you have the key after all."

He had such hope that she could help him. She didn't. It wouldn't take her long to read the journal, but it could take months to decipher it. They only had until Sunday to figure it out. If they didn't, it would be too late for Jairec.

She looked at him and frowned. He looked

peeked. She wasn't sure that was the right word, but his skin appeared paler than it did earlier. "How did my treatment work?" She pointed to his ear.

"I think it's working. It took the edge off."

"But not completely. You need to feed, don't you?"

"You offering?" A teasing feral smile tilted his lips.

"Keep your fangs to yourself. I stopped by the butcher shop. Danny's a friend from school. He gave me a good deal on the pig's blood."

"He wasn't suspicious as to why you wanted it?"

"I said he's a friend. Come on." She headed out of the room and he followed.

"You keep strange friends."

"We're a close-knit family here in Chinatown."

"Hmm, similar to the way it is back home I imagine."

"In Boston?"

"No, I mean Adara."

"You still call Ireland home?"

"It will always be a part of me. Though I can't imagine living there anymore but visiting is grand."

He followed her to where a flight of stairs was located in the back of the shop. The steps led to the apartment up above.

"This is where you live?" he asked.

"Makes it convenient."

"You roll out of bed and start the day."

She looked over her shoulder with a smile. "I like to shower and dress first."

He grinned. "Of course. You smell nice by the way. Good enough to eat."

"I'm not sure that's a compliment, Fang Boy. I might construe your words as a threat." She met his gaze and lifted her brows.

"Not a threat. You don't have to fear me," he added hastily.

"Hmm. Then you might want to do something about your glowing eyes." She flipped on the lights as she went.

"Sorry. Comes with the whole I-am-dead persona."

She went into her kitchen and flipped the light switch, illuminating the room with a warm glow. A nook with three ornate bar chairs separated the kitchen from the living room. Large pictures of Chinese calligraphy adorn the wall above the earth-tone couch— simple, clean and functional. To the left there was a short hall. Her bedroom stood at the end of the hall and to the right was the bathroom.

"Here you go." She handed him a red coffee cup.

"Thank you." He stared at the contents and grimaced.

"Pretend it's home brewed coffee with a splash of cream."

"I wish."

Her brows came together. "I'm curious. Can you drink or eat anything other than blood?"

"Not that I found. I ate the moon cakes I stole from you and threw up."

"Don't tell my grandmother. You'll hurt her feelings." She grabbed a pen and paper from her pencil holder that was next to her phone on the kitchen counter. She slid a bar seat out and sat down to read the journal.

"So it's just you and your grandparents?" He leaned against the counter, facing her.

"Yes, my parents died when I was six."

"I'm sorry."

"Don't be. My parents were happy together. They loved each other and they weren't afraid to show it. They may have had only seven years together, but they lived them loving each other."

"That's a rarity. What happened? How did they ... I'm sorry, I shouldn't be so nosey."

"No, it's okay. A car accident, I would have been with them, but I had a cold and they left me at home with a babysitter."

"It wasn't your time."

She looked at him with a wan smile. "No. Fate perhaps had other plans for me." Her gaze wavered over him, slow seductive. She looked him in the eye. The restless desire there had her heart racing.

He cleared his throat and pulled at his collar as if it had suddenly become inches too small. "The journal's thick." He pointed, changing the subject.

She sighed. "I read fast. Besides we know you have a blood problem."

"To say the least."

"Well it looks like my uncle categorized ailments, treatments and—" The sound of glass shattering downstairs had her on her feet. "What was that?" She took a step toward the door, but he placed a hand on her arm, stopping her.

"You don't know who's down there ... or what."

She chuckled. "Do you think there are more of you around, waiting for me to find a cure?"

"Probably not, but why take a chance. Let me check it out. Stay here." He opened the door as quietly as possible and slipped out.

She waited for about half a second before she ran to the narrow cupboard beside her refrigerator where she kept holiday glasses...among other things. She grabbed her gun then she headed downstairs. "What did he think I did before he entered my life?" she mumbled under her breath.

More shattered glass, which really pissed her off. At the bottom of the stairs, her gaze latched onto the shadowy figures grappled for control, but she knew the taller broader shadow moved like Jairec. He tossed the man against the counter. The shelves teetered and bottles rattled free, falling to the ground like exploding glass bombs.

"Jairec, watch out," she shouted the warning.

The guy came at him, hurdling him to the ground. She couldn't use her gun without possibly hitting Jairec; then again, she couldn't kill him. She aimed and fired.

Curses flew from the assailant as he fell and became still.

"Holy, holy—Did I kill him?" She ran toward the intruder.

"Stop, Autumn!" The warning came a second too late.

The assailant flew to his feet and yanked the gun out of her hand. He held her pressed against his body. "Stay where you are, or she dies." He proved he meant the threat by pressing the barrel against her temple, his fingers itchy to press the trigger.

***

Jairec recognized the timber of the voice and that was startling in its own way. "Tristan?

"Tristan in like he's your brother?" Autumn asked.

Jairec flipped the switch on the wall, flooding the room with light. Tristan squinted his eyes, but he didn't ease his grip on Autumn.

"Aye. It's my no-good brother. Let her go, Tristan and tell me where in the hell you've been?"

"I could say the same about you brother." He jerked his chin at him.

Jairec sensed something was off kilter with Tristan. His muscles tightened as if he sensed a threat, but he didn't understand why. This was his brother. "Let Autumn go."

Tristan hesitated but he gave her a nudge and she ran to Jairec's side. Tristan put the gun down on the counter and held onto his right arm where the bullet had grazed his bicep. Blood oozed from the wound, but he'd live.

"Why didn't you show up at Castagnolia's the other night?" Jairec folded his arms against his chest. He couldn't wait to hear his brother's lame excuse.

"Let's say, I ran into a wee bit of trouble." His mouth flattened into a fine line. "It would be best if you leave town, Jairec."

His brother's words were laced with a warning and his expression filled with uneasy worry. "What are involved in? Let me help you."

Tristan shook his head. "You can't help me." He glanced outside as if what had him spooked lurked there. "You can't fight evil."

Jairec felt the dread slam into him as he realized what trouble his brother was in. "You know of the chiang-shih," he accused. You're the cause of what I've become."

Tristan's gaze riveted to him, his brows furrowing. "What are you talking about?"

"When you didn't show, I went looking for you. The white-haired guy that was with you tried to bash my brains, but instead ..."

"No." Tristan shook his head. His eyes widening as the truth sunk in.

"... made me one of the undead."

"No, how can that be?" Tristan backed away,

running his hand through his hair, his expression changing from confusion to concern.

***

Autumn detected the same rolling speech in each man, indicating they were indeed brothers. Tristan stood a few inches shorter than Jairec and that was not to say they weren't both tall. Tristan's hair was light. Jairec's was dark, but they both inherited the same eye color, whether from their mother or their father she didn't know. "It's nice that you two are having a family reunion, but what is your brother doing here? Why did he break into my shop?"

Jairec crossed his arms across his chest. "Answer the question. I'm curious myself."

Tristan chuckled. "I could say the same of you."

"I was invited."

Tristan's brows lifted. He looked at Autumn and she took a step back not liking how his fixed gaze licked over her.

Her sight landed on where his wound should have been, but the skin was unmarred. "Holy, holy ..."

Tristan realized where her gaze had landed, and he glanced at his arm. "Oh bugger." He hissed as he lunged toward Autumn, but Jairec was quicker and he threw a punch. Tristan flew through the air landing hard on his back, but before Jairec could grab him again, he scrambled to his feet.

"We'll talk later, Jairec to be sure, but I'll leave you with a warning: The Dragon parade will be your doom. Don't be a bloody tap and try to save the day." He fled into the night without turning back.

"Tristan!" he called, running after him. He stood at the door, scanning the street, but his brother had already receded into the night.

Autumn moved beside him. "He's like you, isn't he?"

He turned to look at her. "No, Autumn he's not. The poor sod's tasted human blood."

Chapter Ten

After his confrontation with his brother, Tristen made his way back to the warehouse, keeping to the shadows. He needed to think, and he didn't want his brother finding him without a plan in place.

He paced the large room with the timber beams and poor lighting. The windows had been painted black to keep the sun's rays out. It was dark and damp like a cave. A perfect layout for the nightmare he was living. He was antsy and frustrated with how the events had played out. He whirled on the white-haired man. His Asian eyes a bottomless pool of silver over black, giving them an unsettling appearance of doom. He went by the name Heng. Whether this was his true name or not the name meant eternal, being a chiang-shih he qualified. "I told you I wanted to keep my brother out of this. We had a deal."

"You left me no choice. You brought him here and he wouldn't stop looking for you." His voice lowered and his gaze locked onto him.

"Once he found you— *and you know he would have*—he would know you were different. I couldn't risk it. If I'm to raise an army, we need to be discreet." His shoulders lifted in a shrug as he examined his long sharp fingernails. "I could have drained him, but I brought him over to our side instead. I thought you'd be pleased."

Tristan didn't voice what he thought of this plan. He knew his brother. Even cursed, he could bet the man still held onto his code of ethics. Sainted Jairec always did what was right. He would never be one of them in spirit. In the end, Tristan knew he would have to eliminate him. He threw up his hands in frustration. He hadn't wanted this for his little brother. Like always, he'd dragged him into his mess, but this time he didn't see a way out. "What if Jairec refuses to join us?"

"He will. They all eventually seek our protection. He'll only be able to keep the temptation at bay for so long, but it will become too unbearable. He'll make his first kill and we'll own him."

Tristan swallowed back the sickening lump in the back of his throat. He had yet to make his own first kill. Heng had supplied the blood source thus far. He didn't want to think of where he had gotten it or whose it was.

"Chinatown will be ours." His maniacal laugh grated on Tristan's nerves.

Tristan knew Heng was mad, but he'd conjured him up and now he had to deal with him.

When Tristan had been fired from his job at Old Treasures, an antique store located in the heart of Chinatown, he went to the pub and drank himself into a stupor. Then he did something even dumber, he went back to the antique shop he'd been fired from and broke in. He stole the urn that had arrived earlier that day with symbols he didn't understand. He recited the passage attached to it, not realizing the words sealed his fate.

Heng appeared in a cloud of smoke as if he'd released a genie from a bottle. Heng promised a way to get even with his old boss. He promised him power where no one would bother him. He promised he'd live forever. Tristan agreed, selling his soul to damnation. Now sober, eternal life didn't sound so promising. "My brother was with a human," he told him.

"Yes, I know."

"You knew?" He ignored the quick twist in his gut. "Is this why you sent me there? I thought I was to steal a book or was that a lie too?"

"No, but I don't think we need to worry about it. Jin was the sorcerer. If he had taught his niece, I wouldn't be talking to you now."

Tristan narrowed his eyes. "You wanker. You sent me there as the guinea pig to see if I would be zapped into dust."

Heng laughed. "Why of course. You didn't think I would risk my own neck, did you?"

65

Chapter Eleven

Jairec helped Autumn clean up the shop, putting it back to some sense of order. He boarded the door where the glass had been broken. Autumn would call someone in the morning to fix it.

He turned toward her. She had held up well through all the preternatural business, but it was finally taking its toll. She hugged herself as if she could keep the last thread of her sanity intact. "Autumn?" She met his gaze and her green eyes pooled. He was at her side, pulling her into his arms. "I'm sorry. I shouldn't have brought this to your doorstep. I'll leave. Tristan mentioned the last parade. Whatever is happening will happen then. I'll find my brother and—"

"Shut up, Jairec." She leaned up and kissed him, startling them both. Her gaze met his as if waiting for him to make the next move.

Not exactly what he expected, but he wasn't going to complain. Even in his undead state, it seemed he was still a bloke and she was one attractive woman. His hands went around her waist, pulling her closer. His hands gripped a fistful of her dark hair. His gaze wavered over her features to make sure this is what she wanted. Her eyelids fluttered close and her lips parted. That was all the encouragement he needed. He slanted his mouth over hers, planting a searing kiss.

She pulled at his shirt, rubbing her hands beneath the fabric. He groaned. Her hands tortured him with pleasure. He wanted her and if he could believe the way her hands moved over him, she wanted him, too. He leaned back, brushing her hair away from her face, forcing her to look at him. "Are you sure, luv? Because you know I'm not a saint and now would be the time for you to tell me to back off."

"I don't want you to back off. We could die tomorrow. Well, I could die tomorrow. You could become the undead forever. I want someone to hold me tonight. Make love to me. You can still ... you know do that, can't you." She glanced down and then up to meet his gaze once more.

"Uh ... I believe so. The equipment seems to be working exceptionally well." He stepped back and shoved his hands in his pockets. He hadn't met a girl who spoke her mind, on whatever it might be. He liked it. He liked her. He'd been drawn to her from the beginning as if destiny led him to her.

"Make love to me, Jairec."

He wanted to. Boy did he want to; however, he had to think of her safety. What if he lost control and bit her? He could kill her.

"I trust you," she told him as if she read his mind.

"I don't know if I trust myself."

"I trust you," she said again, pulling his hand out of his pocket and clasping it. "My grandmother says there are no coincidences. Fate brought you to me."

He had thought the same thing a second ago. "What if it was to do you harm?"

She tilted her head to the side, her mouth curving into a smile. "Never. I feel more alive when I'm with you."

He shook his head. "That's not good. A dead man makes you feel alive. What is wrong with this picture?"

"Tell me what is right? Everything's been turned upside down." She leaned up and kissed his cheek. "Tell me you don't feel it."

"There's a connection no doubt. I've never felt this with anyone, and if we had met before all this happened, I would have pursued you like there was no tomorrow."

"There may not be."

"Be serious, Autumn. I have nothing to offer you. There's no future for us."

She nodded her head and took a deep breath. "You can promise me tonight."

"I've learned the night is a different world, one that should be feared by mortals."

"I'm not afraid of you." There was impeccable certainty in her voice.

Her honesty, her aura, the feminine scent of

her had hooked him from the start. Now she laid her heart out for him. "You should be afraid ... very afraid." He allowed his gaze to smolder with desire, but it was meant to warn her of the power he held in check, but she looked at him as if she saw something else ... as if, she saw a good and honest man. "Autumn—"

"I trust you."

"Don't." He closed his eyes and breathed deeply. Big mistake.

"I trust you."

He could smell her. She was fresh and clean with sexy undertones that made him crave a taste of her, not her blood, but her. He wanted to touch her. He wanted to feel her lips again and feel the softness of her hair.

"I don't take sleeping with a man lightly," she told him.

His eyes snapped open. "I never thought ..."

She shook her head. "I wanted you to know."

He cupped her face. "To be sure, I don't take sleeping with a woman lightly either."

"Good to know." Her green eyes held his with longing and he felt his resolve slipping. "Jairec?"

"Hmm?"

"Are you going to kiss me again or not?"

"I shouldn't." He met her lips anyway. Just like the first time he kissed her, he felt the surge course through him. The fiery want to taste every inch of her consumed his actions. He had waited a lifetime to find her. He knew her touch, knew what she craved. It was as if she was his already.

She offered her hand and he clasped it −a lifeline to her world. She led him back upstairs and to her bedroom.

He drew her into his arms and exploited her mouth for all it was worth. His lips wandered over her cheekbones, her chin. He nuzzled her ear and nipped her neck, but he didn't draw blood. She inhaled deeply, but she didn't pull away. He would be careful with her. He wouldn't hurt her. He took her mouth once more and those invisible bonds that drew them to each other tightened a notch more.

He could hear the heightened beat of her heart when he tugged at the hem of her T-shirt. He pulled it over her head. Other clothing followed: jeans, panties, bra and his jeans and boxers added to the pile until they stood before each other in all honesty.

He eased her back toward the bed, pulling back the covers before they fell onto its featherlike softness. He caressed a trail down her arm until he cupped her breast, his thumb skimming over the tip of her nipple. He was fully aroused, desire coursing through his swollen and rigid member. He wanted her now. He wanted to bury himself deep inside her and ride her hard and fast, but he held back not sure of his strength. He reminded himself she was human.

She was fragile.

She trusted him.

He would be damned if he didn't make their first time, perhaps their only time together memorable. He trailed kisses down the length of her. His mouth tasting the sweetness between her legs, stroking and suckling until he felt the sensitive piece of flesh swell with excitement.

"Now Jairec." She drew her fingers through his hair. "Now."

He shifted and with one quick move entered her. She gasped and he stilled. When she wiggled her hips, he realized he hadn't hurt her. She wanted him as much as he wanted her. A growl erupted from the back of his throat, as he possessed her body, immersing himself deeper and deeper, melding them as one. She held onto him as she rode with him. Their gazes locked as they took the tumble over the edge and waves of pleasure rippled through them. He never knew he could love someone so completely in such a short time, but he did. He loved her. That wasn't good. He had no right. He tried to pull away, but she wrapped her legs around him and held him close. He looked at her. She caressed his face, rubbing her thumb over his lips.

"I love you, too."

She read him so easily. "Damn it, Autumn, you shouldn't, but God help me, I do love you." He leaned down and kissed her.

For tonight, all the nightmares of the last

few days were kept at bay, but time marches on and death doesn't wait.

Chapter Twelve

Autumn awoke to find Jairec dressing. The sun hadn't risen yet and the coolness of the morning made her shiver. She pulled the sheet around her. "Where are you going?"

He put on his sweatshirt and turned toward her. "I didn't mean to wake you. I ..." He looked away, swallowing hard.

Then she understood. She reached for his hand. "It's okay." He met her gaze again. "I know you have to feed." She didn't ask where he fed or on what. For two days before she met him, he'd been fending for himself.

He leaned down and kissed the top of her head. "I'll see you in a few hours. I'll try to meet you back here, but if you need to leave, please don't wait. I'll head over to your booth."

She nodded, wanting to cling to him, but knowing she had to let him go. "Be careful."

He gave her a whisper of a smile before he slipped out the door. She must have drifted off to sleep again for the next thing she knew her phone was ringing. She leaned over and picked it up. Her voice croaked out the word, "Hello."

"Autumn? Thank goodness. I thought something was wrong."

"Loann, what is it?"

"You haven't opened the shop and I needed to bring the supplies over to the booth."

Autumn sat up and looked at the clock. "Holy, holy, I didn't realize how late it was. I overslept." She threw off the covers. "I'll be right down. Give me a sec."

She grabbed her robe and shoved her feet into her slippers. She ran downstairs and opened the door to find Loann and Yi there, too.

"You're not dressed," Yi stated the obvious.

"Yeah, well I just woke up. I don't usually sleep in my work clothes."

He harrumphed.

Loann hurried to gather what was needed at the booth.

"What happened with the door?" Yi nodded toward the boarded-up portion where Tristan had broken it to let himself in. Funny, the guy taught Jairec how to pick locks, but he broke her door to let himself in. Had he been warning her to run? Tristan didn't know Jairec would be there to protect her. Maybe Jairec's brother wasn't as lost as they thought.

"Kids," Autumn stated. "A ball hit it and shattered the glass." The lie flew off her tongue with ease. It was to protect them. She justified her actions. The less they knew of what was going on the better.

"I have everything," Loann announced. She held the box and looked from Yi to Autumn, obviously feeling the tension. "I'll meet you at the booth. Hopefully Bruce will show up today. By the way, did you hear from him?"

Autumn cringed. She'd been preoccupied and had forgotten to call him again. "No, but I haven't checked my messages yet. I'm sure he'll show up sooner or later."

"I don't know why you keep the runt." Yi leaned against the counter. "If he were my employee—"

"He's not." Autumn narrowed her eyes and he shrugged. She looked back to Loann. "I won't be long."

"Don't rush. It's foggy out, the worst I've seen in a long time," Loann told her. "The tourists won't surface until this burns off."

"I'll wait for you Autumn, so we can walk together," Yi offered.

"No, go on with Loann."

He hesitated.

"I'm fine, Yi. I haven't had any trouble."

"The door makes me think differently. What are you hiding?"

"Nothing."

His dark eyes narrowed. "You're lying."

"Excuse me."

"Something's going on with you."

She pulled the robe around tighter. "Nothing is going on."

He grabbed her chin and tilted her head up. She pulled away and glared at him.

"You should tell your boyfriend not to bite so hard next time," he sneered.

Her hand flew to her neck. "Get out Yi."

Loann shuffled her feet and chewed her lower lip. For a second, her gaze locked with Autumn's.

"Who is he?" Yi demanded to know.

"It's none of your business. I don't owe you an explanation."

His nostrils flared as he took a deep breath. "You deny me your attention, but you sneak around with someone else. Makes me wonder why?"

"I'm not sneaking around. Now if you don't mind, I need to get dressed."

Yi stood there the muscle in his jaw working as he clenched his teeth. Without another word, he whirled around and stormed out the door. Autumn let out a sigh of relief.

Loann stared at her. "Is it that man who came by the booth yesterday? The good looking one who was all mysterious like."

"We're ... friends."

Loann smiled. "Friends? That's sure one friendly bite he gave you."

"Yeah, I'll have to talk to him about that." She frowned. She'd better wear something with a high collar. Her grandparents were old fashioned. They wouldn't approve of her letting Jairec spend the night. No matter what the circumstances were. She'd never been so bold. She couldn't explain the connection she felt for Jairec. She only knew it was right.

"George asked me to marry him." Loann broke through her reverie.

"Oh Loann, I'm so happy for you."

"Our parents were happy with the match. They had our astrology charts mapped. We're compatible, but I already knew we would be."

"Hmmm."

"Would your grandparents approve of your young gentleman?"

Autumn knew Loann only tried to help. Would her grandparents like Jairec? If he hadn't been cursed to be one of the undead, perhaps. Would they like her to marry Yi? Most definitely. Yi came from a good Chinese family. He owned his own business. Not that she needed him to, but he could provide for her. Whereas Jairec was Irish, like her father had been. Her grandparents would be reminded daily of how her father stole her mother from them. Jairec also lived and worked in Boston. Oh and let's not forget, he's cursed. She pursed her lips together. "Our relationship is complicated."

"Most are, Autumn. If you want my opinion, I go for the dark mysterious guy. Yi is too intense for me. Go shower and get dressed. Later, you can tell me about your guy."

"I'll bring us some coffee."

"Good. Extra sugar for me," Loann said as she walked out.

Autumn stood at the door until the fog swallowed Loann's slim form. She clutched her robe. Her eyes flickered warily through the thick ooze of mist, having a creepy feeling of being watched. She could feel the animosity as if the fog was a live entity and it waited to devour her. She took a step outside her door, not able to resist the pull. She teetered on her feet.

"Come." She heard the call, but it was inside her head, not a voice anyone else could hear.

Her subconscious screamed for her to resist. "No!" She snapped free of the psychic pull, falling back into her shop. She scrambled to her feet and slammed the door shut and locked it. She took a large gulp of air, waiting for her heart to slow to a normal rate. What waited for her out there? What did it want?

Chapter Thirteen

Loann's thoughts drifted to George. He was going to meet her at the booth later on today. She loved the way his hair fell over his brow and the way his smile would make her heart beat faster. She loved him with all her heart, and she prayed Autumn would know the same happiness.

Her lips curved. The way the guy at the booth had looked at Autumn was surely sinful. He looked like he wanted to devour her, and Autumn's gaze hadn't been so innocent either. She wondered who the guy was. She never saw him before yesterday and yet the two seemed like old friends. She chuckled. Friends? No, they were more than friends, if the love bite Autumn sported was any indication. She couldn't wait for Autumn to tell her all about him.

The temperature dropped and she shivered. The weather was strange today. It was often foggy, but not this dense. She could barely see more than a few feet in front of her. A whisper of unease teased her senses as she slowed her pace, not wanting to trip and fall. She'd have a heck of time finding all the items she carried in her box if they were sprawled all over the street.

She hummed a tune, trying to ease the tension building inside of her. She walked these streets her whole life and hadn't been afraid, but she had an uneasy feeling as if she were entering something forbidden. Then she heard something whistle by her. Something big, fast ... She stopped in her tracks and looked around her, but the fog was so thick she couldn't see more than a few feet in front of her. Now she wished Yi hadn't stormed off angry and had walked with her. "Who's out there?" Her voice quavered.

"Who's out there?" a voice mimicked like a perverted echo.

A scream clawed its way up her throat, but she bit it back. She clutched the box and ran. A dark shadow whipped around her and her long hair flew into her eyes. She dropped the box and ran faster. "Help!" She looked over her shoulder, but she couldn't see what pursued her. Where was everyone? Why wasn't anyone else on the street?

"Help me!"

"Help me!" the voice echoed back.

She tripped and fell, landing hard on her knees. Tears sprang to her eyes and she couldn't stop shaking. Then a hand appeared in front of her face in an offering. She grabbed hold and he helped her to her feet. She looked up at her rescuer. "Oh, thank God." She chuckled nervously and took a deep breath to calm her nerves. "I think I let the fog spook me." She looked at him again, wondering why he hadn't let go of her hand. Her eyes widened as the truth set in. The scream never left her mouth as he lunged forward, sinking his teeth into her neck.

Chapter Fourteen

The fog had lifted to a ghostly whisper of what it had been in the morning. Autumn carried two coffees in her hands. She took a sip of hers, letting the warmth slide down her throat. "Perfect."

She walked toward her booth only to slow her pace when she noticed the commotion up ahead. The police were roping off an area where her booth should be. Where Loann should be setting up for the day.

Fear slammed into her, making her chest hurt. "Dear God, no." The cups slipped from her hands, falling to the ground. The lids popped off and the coffee splashed over the sidewalk."

"Hey, watch it," someone shouted at her, but she was beyond hearing.

She pushed her way through the crowd, frantic to see who'd been attacked. Her gaze landed on the victim and her hand flew to her mouth, stifling the scream bubbling in the back of her throat. She shook her head in denial. "No, no, this is not happening."

Loann lay still and broken while onlookers

watched, dressed in their Chinese costumes of bright colors of red, yellow, and pinks all trimmed in gold, too festive for the morbid scene.

"What happened?" She didn't know she spoke out loud until someone answered her.

"A wild animal attacked her. Look how her throat is ripped out," the man next to her answered. The gold of his costume glittered in the now surfacing sun.

"Will someone cover the poor girl?" Officer Fong ordered. Fong was in his early thirties and Asian descent. He grew up here in Chinatown. Autumn knew him as a patient. He'd been in her shop for treatment, suffering from stomach problems. No wonder when he dealt with death.

"A wild animal in the heart of Chinatown? It has to be someone's Pit Bull. You hear about these attacks all the time in the news," someone behind her said.

"Then why wasn't there any blood?"

Autumn wanted to scream. She should have been here. She should have told Loann to wait for her and they could have walked to the booth together.

Then a sickening thought hit her. Jairec left her side early this morning. Had he fed? Did he finally lose control and attack Loann? She gasped as the dark thoughts surrounded her. She had trusted him.

She backed away, tears stinging her eyes. She had to get out of here. She had to find Jairec.

Chapter Fifteen

Autumn walked at a fast pace away from where the crowd was gathering. Loann was dead. The blood drained from her body as if someone had siphoned it out. Her throat had been ravished and the authorities played with the idea that a wild animal had killed her. They lived in the middle of the city. What wild animal could have gotten her unless the zoo hadn't done a head count lately and they're missing a lion or a tiger.

Autumn had a better idea and he walked on two legs and had fangs. Loann didn't deserve this. She was supposed to marry George. They even had their astrology charts done. She entered the shop and found Jairec there; leaning against the counter and looking paler than his Irish skin should look. Funny, she thought after he fed, he'd look better. Even the hair, near his temples, was starting to turn white. She didn't remember the white strands being there yesterday.

"Why did you do it?"

His brows dipped over the bridge of his nose. "You told me to meet you here. I know I was late. I should have just met you at—"

"I don't mean meeting me. I'm talking about the woman you killed."

"What?" He shook his head. "I didn't kill anyone. I drank pig's blood, stole it if you must know. For sure, I'm guilty of thievery, not murder." He took a step toward her and she immediately stepped back. He stilled his movements. "Listen Autumn. A part of you must know I didn't kill an innocent or else you wouldn't be here alone with me now."

True. If he was a murderer, he could take her down any time. She knew the beast dwelled within him and she'd have no defense against him if he unleashed it. "What if you're changing? Maybe there's pockets of time you can't remember. How do I know you didn't have a lapse or something?"

"You don't, I'm afraid. You only have my word."

His brogue thickened reminding her of her father. Her shoulders sagged. He was right. She knew in her heart he hadn't done it, but she blamed herself.

"It isn't your fault either, Autumn."

She looked at him, her eyes pooling with unshed tears. "I slept in. I let her go to the booth alone. The fog, I knew something was in the fog."

"What do you mean?"

"I sensed something there as if it were stalking me. I heard a voice ..." She covered her face. "I should have told Loann to come back. I let her go out there and I—"

"Stop." He had her in his arms. "Stop. You're not responsible for her death. You didn't kill her."

She looked up at him. "A chiang-shih did. Her throat was ripped out. If you didn't do it, who? Your brother?"

He pulled away. "I want to believe he wouldn't but when he was here last night, I smelled human blood on him." He ran his fingers through his hair. "Maybe we should end this now." His gaze held hers. "Kill me before I gain more strength. I won't fight you."

She stared at him for a blink of a second. How could she have thought he'd killed Loann? The demon fought to control him, but he kept it at bay. He was strong, but perhaps his soul had been pure to begin with and this was his strength. She took a deep breath and wiped away the tears. "You're so damn dramatic, Jairec."

He shrugged, giving her half a smile.

He was too attractive for his own good. His gaze locked onto hers and he didn't bother hiding the naked desire warming the depths of his eyes.

"You think me dramatic. It must be the Irish in me. The Irish stories never end well."

"You're in Chinatown now buster and we'll see what we can do."

"The girl, Loann, the one who was killed, was she the one I met yesterday?"

"Yes. She's worked with me for the last three years. She was my friend, Jairec."

"I'm sorry. This will be harder on you then. You do realize we need to stop her from rising."

"What do you mean?"

"You see what happened to me. Whoever is orchestrating these attacks, isn't taking precautions to make sure his victims don't rise. My brother and I are proof of that, don't you think? Do you really want Loann to suffer our fate?"

"Better than being dead."

"Autumn, I am dead. This isn't living. I'm dangerous."

"Not to me, you aren't."

He let out a deep sigh. "I don't know why but you keep me grounded so to speak."

"Yin-yang."

"Aye. Good and evil."

"No, I bring out the good in you—balance your existence, stop you from teetering to the dark side and you stop me from suppressing all my feelings."

His mouth curved into a grin and she caught a glimpse of his fangs. "I make you a bad girl."

Heat surged to her cheeks and she knew she blushed. "You've made me appreciate living and ... being a woman."

"Wow, all that from a dead man. Seriously, I think you need to see someone about that."

"I wish you would stop saying that."

"Autumn, it's true. I'd like to say there's a

future for us, but how can there be when you're living, and I'm destined for hell."

"We'll figure this out. Don't give up hope yet." She walked into his arms and leaned against him. "There must be something I'm missing. Something that will help us break the curse."

"Autumn, what is going on?" Chin's voice boomed from the door, the chime overhead, warning Jairec and Autumn a moment too late that they were no longer alone.

Autumn and Jairec pulled apart and faced him.

"Grandfather," Autumn squeaked.

Who is this man?" He eyed Jairec suspiciously before his eyes widened.

"Grandfather, this is—"

"Shush." He waved his hand at her, silencing her. "He's the one you spoke of, the chiang-shih. Step away from him."

"No." She had never defied her grandfather so blatantly before, but the murderous glint in his eyes had her fearing for Jairec's safety.

Her grandfather narrowed his eyes. His face turned a shade of red. He had always prided himself in how well he spoke English and refused to speak anything else, but now he broke into Putonghua, the mainland language of China or better known to the Western world as Mandarin. She had angered her grandfather big time.

She answered him back, hoping she remembered the translation. Her grandfather eyed Jairec again.

Jairec lifted his chin and stood tall. "I mean her no harm, sir."

Chin mumbled a curse under his breath. "Fool. You endanger her by being here. Loann is dead, isn't that proof enough you cannot control who you are."

"He didn't do it, Grandfather."

"No? Then who?"

"We don't know." Autumn looked away.

"But you suspect," Chin insisted.

Jairec spoke up. "My brother started all of this or at least he had something to do with unleashing another being, a stronger chiang-shih who controls him. I will find my brother. I promise."

Chin eyed Jairec as if deciding his worth. "You fight the change well, boy, but in the end you will lose. Your two souls cannot be separated for long. If not reunited, you will succumb to the nature of the chiang-shih."

"I'll leave before then. I need to stop my brother and whoever he's working with."

He glared for a half a second longer, his gaze traveling over Jairec, judging him. Finally, he nodded. "Okay then. I will help to keep that promise."

"Grandfather?" Autumn questioned.

"I know a thing or two about the chiang-shih. Jin and I fought to bring down one of the fiends, imprisoning his spirit in a jar. He went by the name of Heng. If what you say is true, I fear Heng's been released from his captivity."

"You fought with Uncle Jin? When? How?" She shook her head. "What are you talking about?"

"Our family is from a long line of sorcerers. We were to teach your mother, but she wanted no part of it. She ran away with that Irish bast ..." He cleared his throat. "Your father. Then when you came to live with us, we thought we would teach you our ways, so you would know how to keep the otherworldly at bay. We thought there would be time. Then Jin died and I didn't have the heart." He took a ragged breath. "A grave mistake, I see. I will have to give you a crash course."

"My brother said something would happen during the Dragon parade," Jairec offered.

Her grandfather nodded. "Then this is why the fireworks were stolen."

Autumn and Jairec exchanged looks. Jairec lifted his shoulders in a shrug and she shook her head not knowing what her grandfather was talking about either.

Her grandfather clicked his tongue. "Thunder can kill a chiang-shih. The sound radiates through the body, setting off a chain reaction. Boom!" He clapped his hands together, making Autumn jump. "The fireworks may not do the trick, but it would hamper their abilities. Don't you know this chiang-shih?" His gaze landed on Jairec.

"His name is Jairec, Grandfather."

"Is it now?"

"I'm afraid that I'm limited in the

90

knowledge of what I can and cannot do." Jairec told Chin.

"Interesting, an innocent chiang-shih. A first I am sure."

"It wasn't my choice to be one, but I believe my brother embraced the change. He's never chosen his friends wisely. Perhaps he is the one who released this Heng, you've mentioned."

"You've protected your brother, in the past, haven't you?"

"Aye."

"Only this time you are in over your head. You can't save him."

"Grandfather, please."

"What?" He looked at Autumn. "You don't want me to speak the truth. He is up against the first preternatural being, a born chiang-shih. If his brother went willingly, he is already lost to Heng and will do his bidding." He turned his attention back to Jairec. "He is already doomed. Do you understand?"

"Aye." He nodded. His Adam's apple bobbed up and down. "I understand."

Chin eyed Autumn. She fidgeted with the collar on her turtleneck. Even sleeveless it was too warm to wear, and it prickled her neck. Chin's narrowed gaze sharpened, and she let her hand drop. He walked over to her and yanked down the collar.

He then whirled on Jairec who had the decency to look abashed. "You want me to trust you, but you nibble on my granddaughter's neck?"

"I ... didn't mean ..."

Autumn pulled away. "Grandfather, it isn't what you think."

He cursed again and pointed a finger at Jairec. "You not only sneak into my granddaughter's life when you have no right, but you steal her innocence as well. You have no honor."

"Grandfather, stop. I asked him to stay," Autumn defended him.

"He's right," Jairec spoke up.

"What did you say?" Chin looked at him.

"You're right, sir. I should have walked away, but I let my feelings for her override caution. But know this: I would never hurt her."

Chin stood there; his nostrils flared as he inhaled deeply. Then he released his breath in a whoosh. "Follow me," he ordered

Autumn followed too, but her grandfather turned around, halting her. "Just the chiang-shih."

Autumn didn't understand why her grandfather wanted Jairec, but she knew by his stance that she should not question him.

She bowed. "As you wish, Grandfather."

Jairec followed the old man to the back room where they had found the book. Chin eyed Jairec, making him feel like a bug under a microscope. "Why did you come here?"

"The Seer."

"The Seer? Gladys, the old bat is still giving

advice?"

"Aye."

"And what did she tell you?"

"She told me Autumn Moon was my destiny and the end of the festival would be my demise if I didn't drink from the elixir. She told me Jin would have ..." He shook his head. "No, she said I would find the elixir of life at Moon's Acupuncture. I assumed I would need to speak with Jin."

"Leave it to Gladys to be so cryptic," he mumbled under his breath. He looked at Jairec again. "There is gray in your hair. Is this new?"

"Aye, I noticed it this morning."

"It's one of the signs. How do you keep the hunger at bay?"

Jairec narrowed his eyes. "Am I one of your science projects?"

"I want to know if my granddaughter is safe with you," Chin snapped.

"I told you, I would never hurt her."

"You seem awfully sure of yourself." He opened a draw, his hand curling around a knife.

Jairec held up his hands. "Hey, I don't want any trouble."

Chin held Jairec's gaze as he sliced his own palm.

"What the hell." Jairec backed up. His fangs lowered and his eyes glowed red. "You need to get out of here old man."

Chin let the blood drip down his hand.

Jairec's throat rumbled and a growl left his

lips. He swiped away the sweat that dripped down his face. "Why are you doing this?"

"What if my granddaughter is injured in your quest to stop your brother? Can you resist taking her and draining her? You've already nibbled on her neck. Who's to say you won't take a little more next time?"

"I told you, I wouldn't harm her." The blood teased, rousing the tantalizing scent of prey. He wanted to rip the old man's throat out and feast. He leaned down, gripping his knees and forcing himself not to react.

"Look at you. You're pathetic. You can barely hold back."

"Please stop."

"No. You have to face what you've become. You aren't human anymore." With a wave of his other hand, he pinned Jairec to the wall.

Jairec wondered what other powers Chin possessed. He was stronger than The Seer. The way he pinned him as if he was a bug on a corkboard, forcing him to meet his gaze proved he was no match for Chin.

"Smell the blood," Chin teased letting the precious droplets drip down his arm.

Jairec growled again. His fangs lengthened even more. He squeezed his eyes shut, willing himself to fight the urge to sink his fangs into the old man.

"You're a beast."

"You don't think I know this?" Jairec bit out.

"No, I don't. I see the way you look at my granddaughter. I know you've slept with her and I don't like it."

He met the old man's gaze. "Tell me what you dislike more: That I'm a chiang-shih or that I remind you of Autumn's father?" He heard the way Chin sneered at the mention of Autumn's father. Chin had not forgiven Quinn Moon for taking his daughter away. He most likely blamed the man for her death, too.

Chin's face slacked in surprise that he had read him so easily, but then his lips thinned in a frown. "This has nothing to do with Quinn Moon. I want the best for Autumn."

"Then we are in agreement. I love her." He cleared his throat.

Chin stared at him for a blink of second. Then he released him.

Jairec slid to the floor.

Chin took a cloth out of one of the drawers and wrapped his hand. The smell of blood still filled Jairec's nostrils, but it was tolerable. The urge to kill was not so pronounced now.

"Holy, holy ..." Chin tapped his lip. "You love her."

Jairec stood, a smile tugging at his lips at Chin's choice of words.

"Do you find something amusing?"

"I just realized where Autumn gets her spunk."

"Flattery will get you nowhere, chiang-shih."

"It was worth a try. Aye?" He smiled but Chin's face remained stoic.

"You do realize you cannot be with her."

He sighed and nodded. "I'm aware. I will see

her safe and then ... I will rely on you to end my life."

"With pleasure."

Jairec would have preferred if he hadn't seemed so pleased with the prospect.

Chapter Sixteen

Autumn wondered what her grandfather wished to tell Jairec. Why did he want her to wait out here when he said he needed to teach her how to ward off Heng?

"That's it. I want to know what is going on." She marched over to the door, as it swung open. Jairec's right eyebrow rose as if he suspected she'd been eavesdropping. She wished she'd thought of it sooner. Her eyes caught sight of her grandfather's wrapped hand.

"What happened?" She eyed Jairec then her grandfather.

"It is nothing, Autumn. I cut myself is all."

She didn't believe him. She looked at Jairec, but he wouldn't meet her gaze.

"Fine, whatever." She threw up her hands.

"You have other things to worry about," Chin reprimanded. "You need to pack these." He handed her two bottles, a box of bullets, and a wood stake.

"What are these for?"

"The wood stake through the heart will immobilize a chiang-shih and the copper dipped bullets will kill a white haired one."

"And what's in the bottles?"

"Lighter fluid and salt, of course."

Autumn blinked thinking her grandfather had gone mad. "What do we need those for?"

"We must make sure Loann doesn't rise. Heng will want an army behind him. He must have his strength back. If we don't stop him, we'll have a parade tonight all right only it will be a parade of the damned."

"Grandfather, this is Loann we're talking about."

"Loann is gone. What will rise will be a minion with no more personality than a zombie bent on killing. Loann's throat was ripped out insuring death of the human spirit. There will be no communicating with her. What will rise will be a puppet to do Heng's bidding."

"I don't understand. Jairec isn't like that. We could help her adjust—"

"Stop." Her grandfather held up his hand. "I saw Loann. There isn't a ritual to keep her one soul earth bound. The separation was complete, severed without a chance to change her fate. Heng will raise her and he will control her."

She shook her head. "What are we supposed to do with the stake and the bottle. Am I to drench her then stake her?"

"We're going to burn the body," her

grandfather told her as he swept past her.

Chapter Seventeen

They took the long way around, avoiding the traffic from the festival. San Francisco's hills were brutal with its steep inclines. Chin and Autumn walked the hills with ease. Jairec was surprised he could keep up with them. A few days ago, he wasn't so sure he could have, but in his preternatural state, he was much stronger.

Chin pointed out places of interest as they headed for Jackson Street. Jairec assumed it was a ploy to take their minds off what they intended to do.

"The Chinese Hospital was built in 1925 to replace the Tung Wah Dispensary that was destroyed in the earthquake. You know about the 1906 earthquake, don't you?" He looked back at Jairec.

"I believe I've heard of the disaster."

"Did you know the hospital is the first and only Chinese hospital in America?

"No, I don't believe I knew that, sir."

"Bruce Lee was born there, too."

Autumn pulled on Chin's arm. "Grandfather, we're not on a tour of Chinatown or have you forgotten we're on our way to burn Loann's body?"

He shrugged. "Just making conversation."

Jairec slipped his hand in Autumn's. "It's okay. I was on holiday before this all happened. I didn't even have the chance to see the Golden Gate Bridge or Alcatraz."

"Too bad, chiang-shih." Chin shook his head. "They are both a sight to see, but being what you are, you can't cross a body of water."

Autumn frowned and gripped Jairec's hand tighter. He patted her hand. He'd come to terms with what he was, but he feared she hadn't.

They entered the hospital through the front. Sometimes hiding in plain sight was the best course. They looked like they knew what they were doing and where they were headed. No one asked any questions.

They entered the room where Loann had been placed; awaiting an autopsy as if the ripped-out throat wasn't enough evidence as to why she had died. A sheet covered Loann up to her chin, hiding the ravaged marks that killed her. Her dark hair fanned around her, making her skin look snow white.

"She looks like she's sleeping," Autumn commented.

Jairec gripped her shoulder. "Why don't you wait outside and let your grandfather and I take care of this."

"No." She took a ragged breath. "I'll stay."

Chin opened the bag he brought with him. He pulled out supplies and ritual items Jairec didn't recognize, but Chin explained as he worked. "The Taoist priests used to perform exorcisms to remove the negative energy." Chin pulled out yellow strips of paper with red writing.

Jairec's sense of smell told him it was written in blood. "What are those for?"

"The talismans will absorb the evil." He placed the strips on Loann's forehead. "Autumn, sprinkle the salt around the table Loann is laid out on. It will keep her from leaping from it and attacking us." He looked at Jairec. "You might want to step back chiang-shih. It'll also bind you."

He didn't have to be told twice. He stood to the side as Chin and Autumn worked. Autumn handed her grandfather the other bottle she'd been carrying. Chin doused the sheet that covered Loann. The sulfuric smell of the accelerant filled their nostrils.

Autumn strode over to Jairec, linking her arm through his.

Chin spoke the ancient words to purify the unclean spirit from Loann's body. Jairec could feel the power radiating in the room, pressing in on him even though it wasn't directed at him. Then Loann sat up as if she'd been kissed awake. Autumn gasped and took a step forward, but Jairec held her back. "Remember it isn't her."

Loann with the flesh ripped at her neck turned to look at Autumn. She reached her hands toward her. "Save me, Autumn. I'm your friend." Her voice sounded heartfelt, but her eyes were soulless orbs glazed with death.

"Don't listen to her," Jairec told her, pulling her against him.

Chin's voice rose over Loann's as he continued his chant to eliminate what possessed Loann's body.

Stop old man, Loann hissed as she threw back the sheet, revealing her bloodstained and torn clothes. She stepped down only to jump back onto the table with a hiss. She screeched in frustration like a trapped animal searching for a way out.

Chin lit a match and Loann shrieked again, an unearthly shrill that made them cover their ears. Chin threw the match and the sheets caught on fire rising, swirling around Loann until she became a screaming torch of light.

Autumn hid her face in Jairec's chest. He held onto her, his gaze transfixed on the blaze, knowing he would most likely end up like this. He swallowed the lump in his throat as he found Chin staring at him.

With his keen audible range, Jairec heard the commotion first—angry voices. "They're coming," he warned. "We have to get out of here."

"Let's move then." Chin swung open the door and ran out into the hall. Autumn and Jairec were close behind.

"Stop!" One of the two orderlies yelled. One was tall and the other buff. He looked more like a bouncer for a pub than a caretaker at a hospital.

Chin slammed through the emergency doors at the end of the hall. Alarms blared and the sprinklers went off, the smoke finally triggering them. The men behind them cursed as they slid on the wet tiled floor. Jairec slammed the emergency door shut. Chin raised his hands. "Move aside, chiang-shih."

Jairec pulled his hood over his head and ran over to Autumn. She grabbed his hand, squeezing tight.

Chin summoned his power swinging it toward the doors, stopping anyone from exiting. "That'll hold them for only few minutes. So move!" He ran past them. For an old man, he was fast on his feet.

"We'll split up and meet back at Autumn's shop," Chin ordered.

"Grandfather—"

"Do not argue." He looked at Jairec. "See her safely back, chiang-shih."

"Don't worry."

"Jairec, we can't let him go alone. What if he's caught?"

"I have a hunch your grandfather has a better chance of escaping than we do." He took hold of her hand and hurried down the street. He heard the doors break open and knew the men from the hospital were after them. They kept going until Jairec couldn't hear anyone following them.

They headed down Grant Ave. with its dragon-entwined lampposts, intending to go straight to the shop. Autumn tugged on his arm and he skidded to a halt. Her eyes widened and fear radiated in her gaze.

"What's wrong?" He followed her line of vision and cursed.

Chapter Eighteen

A man dressed in what looked like a period costume of gold and red stood in front of them. His white long hair flowed down his back as if he'd never had his locks trimmed. He could easily be one of the actors for the evening parade, but Autumn suspected otherwise. He stared, his slanted lifeless eyes a shade of silver over black. He tilted his head to the side and his mouth slid into a smile that made Autumn's skin crawl. Jairec pulled her closer to him and she felt safer. A strange feeling since she should fear Jairec with his bite-you-on-the-neck and suck-the-life-out-of-you potential, but this man, this being that stood in front of them was soulless. There was something evil lurking beneath his surface and it scared the hell out of her.

"Do you know the man?" Jairec whispered.

She shook her head. "No, but I saw him in the crowd yesterday. I don't think he's one of the performers."

"I believe he's the bloke who was with my brother the night I was attacked."

"He's not human, is he?"

He inhaled deeply and his nostrils flared. "No. We haven't been properly introduced, but I would bet this is Heng."

The white-haired man was on the move and so were Jairec and Autumn. They followed him down the alley until Autumn pulled on Jairec's arm, drawing him to a stop. "What if he's leading us into a trap?"

"You're right. You stay here." He took a step and she pulled him back again.

"That's your plan. I stay here while you confront the demon from hell."

"Autumn, I'm already dead. You're not."

"Okay you have me in the dead department, but it doesn't mean you should be stupid and let the guy finish the job he started."

He tweaked her nose. "You're cute when you're all fired up."

"Don't try to distract me, Jairec."

He sighed. "I had to try."

She rolled her eyes at his lame attempt. She opened her purse. "I have holy water, salt, and I have this." She pulled out a gun. "It's loaded with the bullets dipped in copper."

"Remind me not to piss you off."

"What I want to know: Do you want to take him alive ... alive as he can be, or do you want me to use the ammo and finish the bastard off?"

"I'd like to take him down, but I want answers too. I want to know if I can reverse this or if you should save one of those bullets for me."

She shuddered at the thought. "We'll keep the guy alive long enough to find out some answers."

"You must promise me you'll stay out of the way and if things get out of hand, that you shoot and ask questions later. If he finishes me off, you'll be vulnerable, so if you see I'm losing, blast us regardless if you could hit me. Do you understand?"

"I'm a good shot, Jairec. I won't hit you."

The corner of his mouth lifted in a lazy half smile.

Boy did she love that grin.

"Autumn, if I don't get the chance to, I want to thank you for all you've done for me."

"Not a big deal."

"Aye, it is." He kissed her soundly and quickly on the lips. "For luck, hey."

"Yeah. Well then." She threw her arms around his neck and claimed his mouth like there was no tomorrow. When she came up for air and met his gaze, he felt a pull low in his gut. "Now that Fang Boy is for luck." Her voice was low, seductive.

"I do believe I like your way better." He caressed her face, wishing they could have more time together without fear that death would steal them away. He gave her a half smile. "Are you ready?"

She nodded. "Ready."

They burst into the room.

Chapter Nineteen

The walls were painted gray and there was a couch in the center of the room. A table and chairs stood under the overhanging lamp. Every window was blackened to keep most of the light out.

"Where's the white-haired man?" Autumn whispered.

Before they could decipher what had become of him. An unearthly wail from above had them ducking as something swooshed over them, knocking both of them to the ground.

Apparently, the white-haired demon could fly. Jairec pulled her toward him, rolling away as the demon screeched toward them. He left her side meeting the next attack by slamming into the demon. They rolled on the ground both trying to gain the upper hand. Autumn held the gun poised and ready to shoot. They were a swirl of gold and gray clothing. She couldn't decide who was winning, but the demon's shriek made her believe Jairec had gotten in few damaging blows.

Then as if the situation wasn't bad enough, four more of the undead appeared from the backroom. The damned flying demon must have called them with his piercing shrill. They're movements were stiff and jerky as if they'd never used their limbs. Two of them wore Hawaiian shirts, one looked dirty and unkempt and the last wore a business suit. It wasn't difficult to realize where Heng had picked up his crew.

"Jairec?"

"Little busy here." He slammed into Heng and he went flying.

"Yeah, well we have company." She backed up a step, pointing her gun.

"Shit." Jairec finally realized what they were up against.

Heng laughed and flew to safety above them, sitting on the rafters. "Meet my children."

"You killed them," Autumn accused.

Heng shrugged his shoulders. "They didn't complain."

"What do you want Heng?" Jairec asked. He stood by Autumn. He kept the minions in his sight. He was ready to fight if he needed to.

"So you know who I am. I believe you're smarter than your brother." His gaze wavered behind Jairec's left shoulder.

Jairec's back stiffened. He whirled around as his brother slammed into him. "Run Autumn. Get out of here."

She hesitated not wanting to leave Jairec. She looked back at the zombie creatures and shot two. Their bodies exploded. Stunned, she stood frozen. Dust swirled around like a tornado before hurdling toward the crevices of the door as if summoned back to where they belonged. She turned to shoot the other two, but Heng screeched and flew down from his perch, knocking her to the ground and her shot went wild, slamming harmlessly into the wall. She scrambled for the gun, but someone kicked it out of her reach. She looked up, her expression changing from confusion to horror. "Bruce, oh my God Bruce, is that you?" He had turned twenty-one last week. He wore his dark hair trimmed above his ears, but now it reached his shoulders with white strands mixed with the black. His almond shape eyes were now dark and lifeless when they usually spoke of mischief and good fun. "Bruce?"

His lips curved. "Hi boss." His voice wasn't his. This wasn't the Bruce she'd worked with. "Do you want me to kiss you like I kissed Loann?"

"What?" She scrambled to her feet. He had killed Loann.

"She'll be with us soon."

Obviously, the Bruce-demon didn't realize they had destroyed her already.

She backed away, scooting across the floor until she felt the gun behind her. Six bullets and she had used three.

"Come to me, Autumn." Bruce's lips sneered and his fangs lengthened.

She gripped the cold metal. As Bruce lunged, she whipped the gun in front of her and pulled the trigger.

Heng snarled and floated toward her. "You will pay for what you've done." She pointed the gun at him and pulled the trigger again, but he disappeared in a wisp of smoke. "What in the heck?" She stood and whirled around. "Where did he go?"

***

Jairec backed away from Tristan.

"You should have listened to me, brother." Tristan stalked him. His strands of hair had taken on the whitish hue.

"What and miss all the fun?" Jairec noticed Autumn took out two zombies and another white-haired vamp, but Heng flew around like a vulture, waiting to pick away the flesh of the remaining contestants. Two more of the zombie creatures headed toward Autumn. She fired two more shots. She was out of bullets and defenseless.

They must retreat. "I hate to break up the party, Tristan, but we have plans. So why not for old time's sake, tell me how I can reverse this curse."

He whooped and slapped his knee. "You're a real wanker, aren't you? Pull your head out of your arse. There's no going back." He glanced at Autumn. "If it's about the lass, take her. Make her one of us and she can be at your side for all eternity. You're one of us now, Jairec. Accept it."

"I'll never be one of you." He charged, head

butting Tristan into the other two zombies. He grabbed Autumn's hand and rushed for the door, bursting out into the bright sun. Jairec cringed and yanked the hood of his sweatshirt down. Tristan had followed but skidded to a halt at the entrance. Shaded by the yawning, he made sure he didn't step into the direct sunlight.

"This isn't over, Jairec," Tristan shouted. "Tonight we finish this, one way or the other." He stepped back and slammed the door shut.

***

Heng clapped his hands and swooped down from the rafters. "Bravo, bravo. I haven't had so much fun in centuries."

Tristan wiped his bloodied lip with the back of his hand. "Fun? You effing freak!"

Heng moved like a flash of light. He grabbed hold of Tristan by the throat, lifting him off his feet. He tilted his head to the side his black lifeless eyes burning into him. "Watch your tongue, minion or I may see fit to cut it out." He let him go, dropping him to the floor where he gasped for breath.

"They almost wiped us out," he choked out.

"Yes. Disturbing isn't it, when a human girl and chiang-shih sucking on animal's blood can take us down. I want them. I want the girl at my side, my queen to rule. The other will be my dog. We'll change him. I'll force him into submission." His gaze bore into Tristan's. "I can be very persuasive."

Tristan knew that already. The bastard liked torture and before the night was through, Chinatown would be screaming in terror. A part of him thrilled at the thought. He shook his head fighting off the urge to kill, but with each cup of blood he drank, it became harder to resist.

"Come," Heng offered his hand, his nails long and pointed reaching for him. "We will drink and regain our strength."

Chapter Twenty

Chin listened to what Autumn and Jairec had to tell him. Jairec stood and paced. Autumn drank green tea but was too agitated to sit still for long. She paced in the opposite direction of Jairec. Then they would turn on their heels and meet in the middle of the room, touching every so often, looking at each other with fear, acceptance and hope for what was to come.

"Grandfather, we need to go back there and finish them off." Autumn stopped moving and looked at him.

Chin shook his head. "Do you really believe it was that easy to eliminate his army? How many did you say there were?" He answered his own question. "Four zombies, two white hairs and Heng flying around but not attacking, did I get that right?"

Jairec and Autumn exchanged glances.

"What are you saying?" Jairec voiced the question.

Chin sighed. "Heng used this as a test to

find out your strengths."

"But we killed his minions," Autumn insisted. "Why wouldn't he stop us?"

"They were dispensable, not ones he would want behind him. They were puppets."

"But I killed Bruce. He was only a kid." The hurt she bore was evident in her voice.

"Bruce was already gone. You said yourself he no longer knew reason. He would have torn your throat open without a thought. He killed Loann without remorse," Chin reminded her.

Autumn knew this, but it didn't make it any easier. "So what do you suggest? The parade is in less than two hours. And what are you going to tell Grandmother? Doesn't she wonder where you've been while she's slaved in the kitchen preparing moon cakes and other pastries for the booth?"

"I keep no secrets from your grandmother."

Autumn lifted her eyebrows. "She knows about the preternatural world?"

"Of course. Did you think her only superstitious? Her precautions were legit. They kept the evil out."

Autumn folded her arms across her chest. "I don't know what to think anymore. Grandfather, you've left me in the dark, vulnerable when I could have been trained. If I had known more, maybe I could have saved Bruce and Loann from the fate they suffered."

Chin stood. "I did my best. I'm sorry now that I didn't do more. Jin warned me this would happen, but I didn't listen. I lost your mother because I forced her to learn our ways. This is why she ran away. I didn't want to lose you, too."

The realization of what her grandfather had to endure hit her. She lost her hostile stance. "I'm sorry, Grandfather. That was unfair."

"Yes, sometimes life is."

Autumn glanced at Jairec who had remained awfully quiet. She whined about her woes, her losses, but what of his? He lost so much more. "Grandfather, do you know if Uncle Jin had a cure for the chiang-shih? Did he know of the elixir of life? I've looked through his journal, but maybe I've missed something."

"We've never come across a chiang-shih with such fortitude to fight the inevitable. There is no cure that I'm aware of. I'm sorry."

Jairec looked away knowing he had only hours. His time on earth was doomed to end then. "Do you mind if I use your computer, Autumn? I want to tie up some loose ends before ..."

He didn't have to say it. Autumn understood. "Sure. Do what you need to do."

The door chimed and Yi sauntered in, his brows rose high on his forehead when he realized Autumn had company. "Did you hear about Loann?"

Autumn nodded. She didn't need this right now. Yi meant well, but she had enough to worry about without having to deal with him. "We heard."

"Someone burned her body." He looked at Jairec sitting behind the counter, working on the computer.

"You replaced Loann awfully quick." His eyes narrowed. "I find it suspicious Mr. Fang that you show up now. You're a stranger who has somehow wormed your way into working with Autumn. How did you manage that?"

"What are you insinuating?" Jairec rose to the challenge.

Not a good sign, Autumn thought. Autumn looked at her grandfather for help, but he just shrugged, leaving her on her own. "Listen Yi, who I have here, is none of your concern."

"No." He whirled on her. "You don't even know him. His name isn't Mr. Fang."

"I know."

"And I ..." He sputtered. He obviously hadn't expected her to state the truth. "You know."

"Let me start over. Yi this is Jairec Connelly and Jairec meet Yi Chung. There, you've both been properly introduced."

She turned away, but Yi's hand shot out, grabbing her wrist.

Jairec growled as he shot to his feet.

Yi's brows drew together.

"Sit down Jairec," Autumn told him. She didn't miss the bit of fang peeking out between his lips. "It's fine." Her eyes widened in warning for Jairec to back down.

"It's fine?" Yi's voice rose. "The man just growled at me. And ... wait a minute. You said his name is Connelly?" Yi harrumphed and shook his head. "I should have known, should have seen the resemblance sooner. Now I know why he looked so familiar."

"What are you twittering about?" Jairec asked with annoyance lacing his words.

"Do you have a brother named Tristan Connelly?"

"What do you know of my brother?" Jairec's eyes narrowed to two slits of red.

"What the ..." Yi backed up a step.

Autumn's gaze darted to Jairec with another warning. He snorted in protest but backed down anyway. She addressed Yi, drawing his attention to her. "How do you know Tristan Connelly?"

"I hired him to unload the merchandise from the trucks."

"Yi owns the antique shop down the street," Autumn filled Jairec in.

"Not only was he a lousy employee, he never showed up on time. He took three-hour lunches whenever the mood struck him, and the dirty sonofabitch, broke into my shop, stealing an urn. I had someone work on the etchings, translating what they meant. The piece would have been priceless."

Chin spoke up now. "Did you say an urn with ancient writing etched onto the side?"

"Yes," Yi answered. "What's going on here?"

"That's how Heng was released," Chin muttered to himself. "It makes senses now." He turned toward Jairec. Your brother must have read the translation out loud. Once done the binding spell would no longer hold him."

"Binding spell?" Yi looked to Jairec then to Chin. "A binding spell for what?"

Autumn placed her hand on his shoulder. "Yi, do you know what a chiang-shih is?"

***

Yi actually took what they told him better than they thought he would. He offered to help destroy Heng. Chin was giving him a crash course of what he needed to look for. Yi was no stranger to the martial arts, and it would come in handy tonight.

"He does this to impress you, Autumn." Jairec had walked up behind her. He didn't startle her. She'd become in tune with his steps.

"Impress me? Why?"

He kissed the top of her head and she leaned back, resting against him. "He's in love with you, surely you know this."

She turned to look at him. "But I don't love him."

He smiled sadly. "I know, but he would—"

"Don't you dare say it. I love you. End of subject, so don't give me some noble speech of doom and how I should go with him."

His lips twitched. "I'm not so noble. I thought maybe you should cut the bloke some slack."

"Oh."

He kissed her frown away. "I love you, too. One day you'll move on, be it Yi or someone else. Just remember to open your heart for the possibility. Hey?"

She didn't answer but wrapped her arms around him.

"Autumn?" She looked back to her grandfather.

Yi stood there, too. His gaze hardened when he looked at Jairec, but he didn't comment on the intimate embrace.

"You'll need to wear gear for tonight."

"Gear?"

"It may save your life or at the very least give you an advantage. Come with me. I'll show you."

Yi and Jairec were left alone in the room. Yi glared at him, but lucky for him he kept his mouth shut.

Jairec shoved his hands in his pockets. Time ticked on making the tension in the room unbearable.

"Autumn was supposed to be mine," Yi finally said.

Jairec clenched his teeth. "She's not one of your priceless artifacts."

"But you'll agree, she is precious."

He'd give him that.

"I don't want her hurt. I don't mean just in the fight tonight. I mean if we make this out alive, I don't want you to hurt her."

"I won't. You have my word."

Yi considered Jairec's answer then nodded. "We're good then."

Yi wasn't such a bad bloke after all. Damn,

Jairec so didn't want to like him. He watched him head toward the back room.

Jairec returned to the computer, determined to tie up loose ends before all hell broke loose.

Chapter Twenty-One

The Dragon parade would begin soon, the town unaware of the horror that awaited them. Jairec would have rather spent a quiet evening with Autumn in his arms, kissing her, making love to her, but a battle against good and evil took precedence. Autumn Moon is your destiny. What did The Seer mean? Maybe he was meant to save Autumn from what Heng had planned. He vowed to protect her. He would do whatever it took to make sure she came out of this alive and unscathed. He glanced at the computer screen in front of him. He was finished here. He logged out.

"It's time," Chin announced.

Autumn walked over to Jairec. "Let me warn—"

He pulled her into his arms before she could finish but backed away immediately his hands burning. "What the hell are you wearing?"

"Sorry, I tried to tell you. I'm wearing a copper mesh vest." She lifted her shirt to reveal the lethal metal. "I'm not superhuman but it

123

will protect me some."

He nodded. "It'll protect you from me, also."

"I didn't wear it to ward you off."

He held up his hand halting her words. "I know, but we don't know what will happen tonight. I'm not sure if I can keep the demon locked inside of me forever. His fingers slid through his hair, where he knew the strands of gray had grown long and thick. "Promise me, Autumn. If we fail, you'll end my life."

She shook her head.

"You have to. Please don't let me turn into a monster feeding on the innocent."

"You won't do that."

"You give me too much credit." He sighed. "Just promise me."

Tears sprang to her eyes, but she gave him a quick nod. "I promise."

Chin cleared his throat, drawing their attention. "I hate to break up the tender moment, but we have a job to do."

Autumn took a deep breath, bringing her emotions under check. She glanced at Yi who stood by her grandfather. He wouldn't meet her gaze. "What exactly is our plan?" Autumn asked.

"We draw them out. Keep the minions from killing our neighbors and the tourists. When Heng is among them, I'll conjure up a thunderstorm."

"What?" Autumn and Jairec chimed in at the same time.

"A thunderstorm. Jin and I banished Heng's

spirit to a container with a binding spell. We buried it, foolishly thinking no one would unearth it. We believed Heng would never be released, a mistake on our part. Thunder is a magical power conjured from dragon's magic. Unfortunately, when we encountered Heng the first time, we didn't realize the significance of it, or we would have used it. It will kill him and all the others that follow under his rule. This will end tonight."

"And what of Jairec?" Autumn held her grandfather's gaze.

He sighed. "There is a chance that he may perish along with the rest of them."

"No." She shook her head. "No, there must be another way."

"Autumn, it's all right," Jairec spoke up.

She looked at him with disbelief. "It's not all right. The Seer sent you to me to help you. Destroying you can't be what she had in mind."

"Autumn."

"No, I don't want to hear it." She whirled around and fled upstairs.

Jairec looked at Chin. "I'll talk to her."

"The thunder may not affect you," Chin told him as he walked past.

Jairec turned to face him. "Why wouldn't it?"

"You haven't killed an innocent. Your humanity is still intact."

Jairec nodded. "Still, she needs to be prepared. Either way, I'm ready to meet my fate."

"Good to know, chiang-shih."

Yi walked over to the stairs, holding onto the rail as he stared after Jairec. "What does he have that I don't have?"

Chin sighed. "Dear boy, he has Autumn's heart."

Chapter Twenty-Two

The band blared, drums beating in time with the thump of Autumn's heart. Jairec went with her to head up the front and Yi went with her grandfather to bring up the rear. She gazed at the people who were her neighbors and friends. They were in danger, but she knew she couldn't yell from a rooftop, begging them to go back to their homes and lock the doors. Even with their superstitious beliefs of placing mirrors on the outside of their windows to ward off evil, they would still think her a lunatic and ignore her warnings.

She patted her purse, which she had slung over her right hip and felt comforted by the feel of the gun loaded with the copper tipped bullets. She glanced at the performers who manned the life-size dragon puppets. The fog had rolled in earlier than usual, hiding the feet of the performers, giving the dragons a surreal appearance as they danced to the beat of the drums, the dragon's faces grinning in frozen delight. They drifted close to the crowd, touching, luring ...

Autumn stopped cold and took hold of Jairec's arm. "I know how he'll do it."

"How?"

"The dragons. They'll take them one by one, under the dragons. The people won't realize their loved ones are missing, until it is too late."

Someone screamed to the right of where they stood. The crowd didn't look alarmed since across from them, teenagers screeched in delight and clapped their hands. Jairec tapped her shoulder and pointed. "Over there." They nudged their way through the crowd. The dragon swept close, swallowing the onlookers as if the beast feasted on its prey. Autumn tried to step back, but the crowd pushed forward. She grabbed onto Jairec's hand, but she was ripped from his hold.

***

"Autumn!" Terror struck Jairec like it had never done before. It spread through him as he watched her disappear beneath the brightly colored cloth. He went crazy then, lashing out, slicing at the material. He had to get to her. He had to save her.

His chest heaved from the exertion and he looked at the damage he wrecked. He realized then he caused a panic. People around him shrieked and moved back.

"It's part of the parade," some fool yelled, and the people stopped.

Jairec throttled the urge to turn on the man

and kill him for his stupidity. The crowd hushed and pointed as if awestruck. Jairec looked over his shoulder. The crowd foolishly watched. This wasn't a performance and yet they stood there waiting to applaud.

Tristan threw off the head of the dragon, revealing more than one chiang-shih with their hair gray and long. The fog still blanketed the ground and he knew it covered the victims the fiends had drained. He wondered how long before the dead rose, hungry and looking to feed?

His gaze locked onto his brother who had Autumn's arms pinned behind her. So much for the copper mesh vest she wore. It looked like she needed cuffed arm gear as well.

Let her go, Tristan," Jairec demanded.

Tristan's mouth curved. "Don't believe I will. Heng wants her. He decided he fancied her at our last meeting."

Now why would she want a guy who has a face like a lap dog? Just give me the girl and I won't kill you."

Tristan's chuckle strummed from his chest with malice. "Why do you care about this human? What's so special about her?"

Jairec gave a careless shrug. He had to remain calm, not act desperate, but it proved difficult when he witnessed the terror in Autumn's gaze. If he could hear her heart pounding in her chest, his brother could hear it, too. "I owe her. She gave me shelter when I needed it."

"Is that so. You won't need shelter if you join Heng. We'll rule California and beyond. He has big plans where a chiang-shih will head each city. We'll be gods."

Jairec wondered why the nuts always wanted to take over the world. "Sure. Why not? But a god must have a goddess at his side." He looked at Autumn. "I claim her."

"Uh uh. Heng wants her for himself. He's the boss."

"I want her at my side."

Tristan stared at him as he considered his offer. "Hmm, interesting." He leaned forward and Jairec resisted the urge to lunge. Tristan sniffed Autumn's hair, inhaling deeply. Autumn closed her eyes. "Ah, I see why you're so interested in her. She reeks of you, Jairec. You've been shagging her, haven't you?"

"Piss off. That's none of your concern now is it?"

"Tsk, tsk. Is that anyway to speak to your older brother?"

"Do you mean the wanker who allowed me to be turned into a chiang-shih? That brother?"

The crowd behind him gasped. He didn't think his language caused the shock. He turned as the shadow swooped overhead, coming dangerously close. Jairec ducked. Then Heng hovered, descending like a savior when he was truly the prince of evil. He wore red and gold vestments for the shindig. His sallow skin took on a darker hue of green. He shook a long, pointed fingernail at him as he lowered himself to the ground.

"You might want to clean up your mouth, Jairec. You're scaring the tourists." Heng clicked his tongue at him. He then turned his attention to Autumn, tilting his head to the side, his fangs lengthening. He traced her jaw with his nail. "So pretty."

Jairec didn't dare look around but he wondered where Yi and Chin were. Where were the dragon thunderbolts to wipe this bastard out?

Autumn jerked her head away and stepped back, but Tristan thrust her forward again. Autumn glanced at Jairec. She blinked and calmness overtook her composure. A second before she lunged, Jairec realized what she was about to do. "Nooooo!" he screamed, but it was too late.

She threw herself around Heng, holding him in a bear hug. Heng cried in pain as the copper burned through his clothing, his skin sizzling on contact, the putrid rot scenting the air. Heng screeched, twirling up, trying to dislodge Autumn's hold. Jairec leapt forward and grabbed onto Heng's feet, anchoring him. He didn't know how long he could hold onto him, but to let go wasn't an option.

"Get them you fools," Heng demanded, thrashing to shake Jairec off his leg.

Tristan slashed at Jairec's midsection with his long nails, but Jairec used Heng to pull himself up, kicking Tristan in the face. He fell back, landing into two of the other minions, causing them to lose their balance. They hissed and spit, trying to dislodge their tangled limbs.

The crowd applauded. Jairec thought the fools deserved to die. Didn't they recognize a real threat?

Darkened clouds gathered overhead hastening nightfall. "Chin's magic," Jairec mumbled under his breath. He wished the old man would work faster. Heng spiraled up, hovering above the ground. He was too high to let go now. He might survive the fall, but he wasn't sure if Autumn could. He thought about going for her gun in her purse, but it would prove too risky. He could shoot her. He hoped she could hold on. He looked down below, wondering if any of the other vamps could fly. Tristan looked like he wanted to give it a try. He stood ready for battle, but before he leapt off his feet, Yi had come to the rescue. A right kick landed against Tristan's skull.

Jairec climbed up Heng's leg like it was a rope. If he could grab Autumn, he'd take her with him, bracing her fall and taking most of the impact.

Heng desperate to free himself jabbed Autumn with his nails, but the mesh held, burning his hands. He grabbed her face, forcing her look at him.

"Close your eyes, Autumn. Don't look at him," Jairec warned, but it was too late.

Her eyes glazed and her grip lessened. Heng held her away from him. Jairec snaked out his hand to grab her, but Heng tossed her away.

Her shirt feathered through his fingers. Jairec watched in horror as her body hit the ground. She didn't move. A rage like he never known before welled inside of him. He wanted Heng dead. Now.

Heng's wounds healed, giving him back his strength. He grabbed Jairec by the hair and hauled him up to eye level. "I would have given you a seat of power, but you've deceived me." He raised his hand to give a fatal blow, but the first rumble of thunder broke through. Heng hesitated. Jairec took the advantage and slammed his fist into Heng's face. Bone crunched and he knew he'd broken Heng's nose. He let Jairec go and he flayed his arms around, trying to stop his fall. What he would have done if he could fly. He landed hard but tucked and rolled. He felt bruised but he leapt to his feet, waiting for Heng to attack again.

The rumble in the heavens clamored. Heng covered his ears and screamed. Tristan and the two other vamps did the same. Yi took his dagger and rammed it into one of the minions then spun, hitting the other demon in the chest. Both exploded into dust on impact.

Jairec waited for the thunder to affect him, but nothing happened. He could still function. He grabbed a hold of his brother as another thunderclap roared in his ears. Tristan's screech joined Heng's and the look on his face couldn't have been worse if Jairec had driven a stake through his heart. "It wasn't supposed to be like this, Jairec."

"I know."

"Forgive me, brother." He stepped away.

The thunder rolled again.

Tristan covered his ears. His whole body shook so fast his features blurred. An ear-shattering explosion of thunder roared louder, longer. Tristan exploded as if triggered by a bomb. The blast hurdled Jairec backwards, Yi slamming into him.

Heng spun around and around. The whirl of wind brought up debris and dust until he swirled into a black funnel. Heng's features blurred into the twister and his bellow pierced the air. People ran for cover as storefront glass shattered. The earth shook. Jairec forced himself to his feet and moved toward Autumn who lay helpless. He covered her body with his, ignoring how the copper burned. He would protect her.

The thunder roared again like a mighty dragon, lashing out at its prey. The wind hurled dirt into Jairec's hair, eyes and between his teeth. Then the dark clouds moved aside and the last of the sun's rays shone through like a laser beam. The funnel ignited sending sparks of shooting light like a firework show. The last sparks dwindling into smoke and ash.

The roar of absolute silence spread. No one moved and no one breathed.

Jairec rolled away from Autumn. His sweatshirt burned from his body and his flesh was blistered and raw.

Yi walked over and leaned down to look at

Autumn.

"Is she all right?" Jairec choked out.

"She's breathing."

"We have to get her to the hospital."

Yi's gaze traveled over him. "You could use a doctor yourself. You don't look so good."

Jairec wanted to curl up in a ball, but he needed to secure Autumn's safety first.

"Are they all dead? Did we wipe them out?"

"The last one blasted away with Heng."

Chin pushed his way through the crowd and offered a hand to Jairec, yanking him to his feet.

"A little worse for wear, but you survived, chiang-shih. I'm impressed." He leaned down to look at Autumn.

"Survived? That's up for debate," Jairec mumbled.

"Hmm. We'll argue the matter later." He looked over his shoulder when he heard the whistles and shouts from the police to back up. "Help me pick up Autumn, Yi. We must move before we're forced to answer questions."

Chapter Twenty-Three

Autumn's eyes fluttered open and she sat up with a start.

"There, there now." A nurse dressed in white pants and a blue hospital shirt approached her. "I'm glad you're awake."

The smell of disinfectants hit her nostrils first, followed by the smell of coffee and food. Her gaze landed on a covered plate set on the turnout tray that was attached to the bed. A steady beep drew her attention to a monitor bolted to the wall. Then her gaze landed on the IV bag hanging from the silver pole. She closed her eyes and rested her head against the pillow, trying to remember what happened.

"I'm in the hospital." Her mouth felt thick and dry, making the speech difficult. "Water, please."

The nurse poured water into a plastic blue cup and held the straw, while Autumn lifted her head to sip. The liquid ran cool down her parched throat.

The nurse was young with her dark hair pulled back away from her face.

"Jairec. Where's... Jairec?" she licked her

136

lips.

"Jairec?" the nurse asked.

"Yes. Dark hair... man... not Chinese... my age."

There was a nice-looking man with gray hair who sat by your side. He had been badly burnt, but he wouldn't let anyone tend to him. He disappeared before I could summon the doctor."

Her brows furrowed. Gray hair? Was she talking about Jairec? Had he turned? "I have to go." Autumn grimaced when she pulled the IV out of her arm.

"No, what are you doing. You can't leave."

Autumn ignored her, throwing her legs over the side of the bed. She forced her limbs to move and hurried over to the closet. She was relieved to see that her clothes were there, the damn copper mesh and all. Jairec had risked his life to save her. If his hair was snow white, he was slipping.

The nurse had run out into the hall, yelling for the doctor.

Autumn removed her gown, her limbs waking up as she shoved on her clothes.

Once she donned her shoes, she glanced inside the closet to see if she had everything and her gaze landed on the vest. If Jairec was burned, he came in contact with the mesh. She swung the closet door shut with a curse.

She walked over to the door and poked her head out. By the front desk, she spotted the nurse talking to a doctor. She hurried the other way, heading for the exit sign and the door labeled with the word stairs. She was too afraid to wait for the elevator and have someone stop her. She needed to find Jairec.

Chapter Twenty-Four

Jairec lay close to death—again. After he made sure Autumn would be fine, he came back with Chin not sure where else he could go. Chin took precautions. He locked him in the room above the pastry shop. Salt and wood charms lined the doors and windows. He wouldn't escape. He'd drunk the pig's blood, but it didn't help. It didn't restore him. It was as if the copper poisoned his system, weakening him. His hair had turned as white as the moon's lighted surface. His skin a sallow color, but at least it hadn't turned green.

He heard a commotion, raised voices from the other room. He heard Autumn's voice.

"I don't care grandfather," she said as she threw open the door, slamming it against the wall.

He sat up in bed. She stood in the threshold her gaze locking onto his. She was so beautiful, a vision for his weary eyes. It seemed a lifetime ago when he had first kissed her, when he had first made love to her.

"Don't leave me, Jairec." She took a step toward him.

"Don't come too close," he warned.

She didn't listen.

"Please, Autumn. I don't want to hurt you."

"You won't." She threw her arms around his neck, hugging him.

He chuckled. "You've always given me too much credit."

"I don't think so. You're honorable. You risked your existence to save me. Now look at you." Her voice caught in her throat. "I've killed you because of that copper mesh I wore."

"If you hadn't worn it, you would have died. You should be in the hospital now. I can't believe they let you go."

She didn't say anything.

He pushed her away so he could look at her. "They didn't let you go, did they?"

"I'm fine."

"You need to go back."

"No."

"Has anyone ever told you, you're stubborn, lass?"

"Yep." She threaded her hand through his hair. "So gray."

"I've looked better."

She chuckled, but her eyes pooled with tears. "You need blood."

"Had some. It's not working, Autumn."

"You need human blood. I can still save you." She rolled up her sleeve and offered her wrist.

He shook his head. "No."

"If you don't, you'll fade into nothing and your soul will be lost."

"If I drink too much, I kill you and condemn my soul anyway. I'll take my chances as long as I know you're all right."

"No, I won't accept it." She stood and stormed out of the room only to return a moment later.

His gaze caught the glitter of the blade. Her grandparents followed her in.

"Stop, Autumn," Chin demanded.

"No, don't do it," Jairec pleaded.

"Maybe my blood is the elixir."

"No, it isn't."

She sliced her wrist anyway. The tangy smell of blood filled his nostrils. His teeth lengthened and his eyes dilated. "No!"

She didn't listen, shoving her wrist over his mouth. He held his breath, clamped his mouth shut, but a small amount of blood seeped in anyway. He couldn't hold back. He grabbed her wrist and drew in the essence of life. He could hear her heartbeat, stronger vibrating in his head, in his chest. He had to stop, or he'd drain her, but the taste was so... He pulled away, turning his head in disgust over his lack of control. Autumn wisely backed away giving him space. He thought he would be all right. He felt stronger more vibrant, but something pulled at him, taking him away.

Autumn screamed. "Don't go!"

It hurt him to see her beautiful face so

ravaged with emotion. He reached for her. "I love you."

What's happening?" She watched in horror as he faded away as if he had never been there.

She fell to her knees, a retched sob vibrating from her chest. "You can't take him. You can't," she wailed to the heavens. "Not him too. You've taken everyone."

"Not everyone." Chin gripped her shoulder and she let him bring her to her feet, folding his arms around her.

Chapter Twenty-Five

It was time to clean up. The Autumn Moon Festival was over, the people of Chinatown would return to their businesses and their way of life like they always did. For Autumn, everything had changed. She didn't want to open her shop, so she left the closed sign in the window. No one would understand that she mourned a man who had been dead when she met him.

She needed to pay bills, check her e-mail. She logged into her computer. She frowned. She had mail from Jairec. He must have sent it to her before they took their stand against Heng. Her heart pounded against her chest as she opened it.

Dear Autumn,

The time draws near that we will have to fight Heng. I can never repay you for your unselfish kindness, your gentle heart. I would love to be with you always, but I fear it is not meant to be, but perhaps you'll think of me once in a while when you look at your website I've designed for you. Click on the link below. I hope you like it.

She clicked on the link and the page opened to Moon's Acupuncture. A beautiful Moon in the background, her bio and information about what she offered. The site was beautiful, but it was the Chinese symbol in the right corner of the page that made her eyes mist.

情人

Soul mate. They were only granted a short time together, but she knew he had been the one for her. He had felt it, too.

A knock at the door broke into her thoughts. She took a deep breath and wiped away the tears. Couldn't they read the sign? She marched to the door and swung it open. "We're clo ..." the words lodged in her throat.

"I'm sorry to be troubling you miss, but I was drawn to this place." His sea-smoked eyes gazed at her and he had hair the color of the devil's black velvet. He stood in the sun's rays and did not flinch or burst into flames.

"Jairec?"

"Aye." His brows furrowed over the bridge of his nose. "You know me then. This will sound a bit peculiar, but I don't know why I'm here and yet ..." His gaze slid over her, confusion lighting his features.

"You're two souls united. You're not dead." She touched him to make sure he was solid.

He chuckled. "No, I'm not dead. Though, the doctors said I should have been." He touched the back of his head. "Someone hit me from behind. You'll have to pardon my behavior my memory is a bit fuzzy."

"You found your way here."

"Aye." He turned a shade of red and his gaze wavered before he looked at her again. "I dreamt of you." He cleared his throat, seeming embarrassed over his confession.

She tilted her head and smiled. "Good dreams, I hope."

"Um ... uh ..."

She stepped toward him and wrapped her arms around his neck. "Perhaps I can jog your memory." She kissed him. He stood stiff and unyielding for a half a second then his arms came up around her, crushing her to him.

They came up for air and he moved a strand of hair away from her face. His gaze locked with hers. "I've kissed you before."

She nodded.

He frowned, trying to remember but only fragments flitted across his mind and he wanted all of it. He looked at her again.

"Do you want to come in?" She stepped away from him, allowing him room.

"Aye, I believe I do." He walked in and closed the door behind him. He didn't know how he knew her, but some part of him sensed he belonged here. "What's your name?"

"Autumn Moon."

The name stirred him. "Autumn." He whirled the name on his tongue. He looked at her again and recognized the longing in her eyes. She walked over to the counter that stood below the shelves that held bottles of herbs and other concoctions. He stepped closer, having the urge to run his fingers through her hair to find out if it was as soft as it looked, but before he could reach her, she thrust a plate of pastries at him.

"Would you like a moon cake?"

"What?" He frowned, staring at the lotus seed cakes.

"It's how we met."

He didn't want pastries. He wanted ... He took the plate from her, setting it on the counter. He drew her into his arms and kissed her, tasting her. Flashes of a life, his life flew at him until he felt dizzy. He teetered and she grabbed a hold of him.

"Jairec, are you okay?"

He placed his hands on the side of her face. "Aye, I'm brilliant." He kissed her again, only this time, everything fell into place.

She pulled away. "You remember."

"Aye. I remember much more, too. It seems you did have my cure after all."

"The elixir of life?" She shook her head. "We didn't figure it out."

"Ah, but you both did."

They turned around at the sound of the voice behind them.

"Grandfather, what do you mean?"

"Autumn gave you her life essence freely and you, Jairec didn't selfishly take all of it. Life is all about balance. The curse was then broken, joining Jairec's two souls once again." He gave him a long sizing up moment before he nodded. "He is a remarkable young man, Autumn. You've chosen well."

Jairec drew Autumn close. He never wanted anything more than to have her at his side. "I'm the one who is grateful."

"And well you should be." Her grandfather agreed. "Make sure you cherish her."

Jairec looked at her, meeting her gaze. God, she had eyes that made him forget to breathe— clear green and trusting. "I'll treasure her forever."

Author's Note:

A few of San Francisco landmarks are the Golden Gate Bridge, Alcatraz Island, and Chinatown. There are cable cars and steep rolling hills with a mix of Victorian as well as modern architecture. The city is surrounded on three sides with water and it is common for fog to roll in like a filmy white blanket, especially during the summer months.

San Francisco's Chinatown is the oldest in the United States. The town draws in more tourists than the Golden Gate Bridge.

The Moon Festival is held in late August or early September. The festival is like a Chinese Thanksgiving with the spirit of gratitude. There is plenty of food and of course, the popular moon cake I mentioned in the story. The holiday is also about the bounty of the summer harvest, the legend of the moon, the immortal gods and the elixir of life.

The Chinese vampire is called the chiang-shih. As legend states they may appear to look human. There are others that are a green color with long gray hair. This is why I used the contrast for the creatures in this tale. The evil vampires looking more like the hideous creature of nightmares. If only all monsters could be so obvious.

The Chinese believe a person has two souls. The superior soul can leave a sleeping body, appear as the body's double and walk the earth. However if the two souls remain separated for long there can be dire consequences.

A chiang-shih is created if the body has suffered a violent death, improper burial or by an incantation. The transformation is thought to take place prior to burial.

People would protect themselves from the chiang-shih by using salt and of course, like most vampire legends, they used garlic to ward off the living dead. A chiang-shih could be chased away by loud noise and it was believed they could be killed with thunder. If the chiang-shih matured to the white-haired stage and could fly, the creature could only be killed by a bullet or thunder. The body could also be cremated.

If you're interested in learning more about the chiang-shih legends, here are a few sites of interest:

http://paranormalstories.blogspot.com/2007/10/chiang-shih.html

http://istina.rin.ru/eng/ufo/text/666.html

http://galleryoterror.blogspot.com/2007/10/chiang-shih-jeff-davis.html

If you want to know more about the Chinese Moon Festival check out these sites:

http://www.moonfestival.org/

http://chineseculture.about.com/library/weekly/aa093097.htm

http://www.chiff.com/home_life/holiday/harvest-moon-festival.htm

http://chinesefood.about.com/od/mooncake/a/moonfestival.htm

A sneak peek of another Karen Michelle Nutt tale...

Moon Shifter

Grayson was near. Intuition told her to run, hide, but she stood paralyzed by a new sensation furrowing down her spine—the beat of desire, strong and unrelenting as she allowed herself to remember when she was human and how Grayson's strong competent hands caressed her body. How could she hate him and desire him, all in one beat of her heart?

Like a vision, he strode into view, tall, lean and sexy with a bit of male animal lurking beneath the surface. She could sense the wolf in him now. So obvious. How had she ever missed it?

His thick-lashed, silver eyes had not seen her yet, but he must know she was near since he moved with caution. His black hair, overly long and sinfully thick framed his handsome-as-the-devil face. He aroused her like no other man had, but now she knew why. He wasn't a man, but a werewolf.

Sinking to a crouched position, she hoped to make herself invisible, but her movement pricked his ears and his gaze riveted to hers. God, he looked good in his black slacks and jacket. She remembered what lay beneath—muscles, firm thighs, tight buttocks, all so male. He was what every woman dreamed of touching…and she had. It didn't matter she was in wolf form. Fire licked through her body as every hormone inside of her came alive. She didn't know if she wanted to tear him from limb to limb or force him to make love to her in whatever form he chose. Maybe she'd do

153

both. She now stood stiff-legged and tall with her ears erect. Her hackles bristled, warning him.

Grayson's eyebrows rose and a hint of a smile tugged at his lips.

He wouldn't be amused if she tore his heart out. She bared her teeth and growled letting the fury roll over her.

"I'm sorry, Sydney." His rich seductive voice reached her even though he had whispered his plea for forgiveness.

Sorry? What did he mean he was sorry? Sorry for what? Then she knew. She'd been too cocky, too enamored and too pissed off to notice he carried a rifle. So, this was how it was going to be. Well, he'd have to catch her first. She whirled around and ran.

She could hear him behind her, fast and sure-footed. A shot whizzed by her ear and she zigzagged hoping the next bullet wouldn't find its mark. He made her into this monster and now he wanted to kill her because of it? Damn it, he was a werewolf, but in the recesses of her mind, she knew she shouldn't be one. Werewolves were forbidden to turn a human into one of them. Grayson was trying to cover his ass no doubt—the bastard. The thought of facing him and ripping him to shreds crossed her mind. Then something sharp pierced her flesh. She let out a howl as her hind legs gave out. She tried to rise, but her body wouldn't obey. Damn if she'd make this easy for him and rolled over. He'd have to look her in the eyes when he ended her life.

He approached her with caution.

That's right, come closer, so I can rip you a part limb by limb. She waited and conserved what was left of her strength.

He leaned down on his haunches.

She lunged, snapping her jaws at him, but he didn't flinch. His brows furrowed and his silver eyes looked pained. How thoughtful. He felt sad he had to murder her. Well, she felt betrayed and hurt that he cared so little for her.

"I'm truly sorry, Sydney," he told her with unmistakable regret in his tone. She might have believed him if he hadn't shot her. Again.

Heart of a Warrior (E-book)

Scáthach is the warrior goddess from the Isle of Skye. When a young boy pleads for the goddess to help his Uncle Trey, his prayers do not go unheard. However, she is surprised to find Trey Brennan, not on a battlefield but in a hospital room, hooked to monitors, his body rejecting a bone marrow transplant. She would accept the challenge and educate Trey in the art of warfare. A war was a war no matter where the battle was held. Be it on the fields of heather with an army or an illness attacking the body. Both held the enemy that needed to be defeated.

Trey Brennan knew he was dying, but he awakes in another realm where the goddess

Scáthach wants to teach him to be a warrior. He is sure he's dreaming, but what did he have to lose? He would train and he would fight. Perhaps his destiny on the Isle of Skye would also change his path in his world.

About the Author:

Karen Michelle Nutt resides in California with her husband, three fascinating children, and houseful of demanding pets. Jack, her Chihuahua/Yorkshire terrier is her writing buddy and sits long hours with her at the computer.

Her Book, Lost in the Mist of Time, was nominated for New Books Review Spotlight Best Fantasy Book of the Year Award 2006. A Twist of Fate was a nominee for Best Time Travel P.E.A.R.L. Award for 2008. Creighton Manor won Honorable Mention P.E.A.R.L. Award 2009.

Her new passion is creating book covers for *Western Trail Blazers* and *Rebecca J. Vickery Publishing*. In her spare time, she reviews books for PNR-Paranormal Romance Reviews.

Whether your reading fancy is paranormal, historical or time travel, all her stories capture the rich array of emotions that accompany the most fabulous human phenomena—falling in love.

Visit the author at: http://www.kmnbooks.com

Stop by her blog for Monday interviews, chats and contests at:

http://kmnbooks.blogspot.com

Karen Michelle Nutt

Time Travel and Otherworldly Romances

Lost in the Mist of Time

Dougray Fitzpatrick has buried one wife and vows to never love again—but destiny has other plans for this 16th century Irish Lord. During a battle, a mist separates Dougray from his men and casts him into the future. Dougray must return to Dunhaven and to his century, but Aislinn Hennessy follows him into the mist, leaving him no choice, but to take her home with him.

Conspiracies, feuds and unexpected violence are commonplace threats, but along the way, Aislinn and Dougray discover a surprise neither one expects: a chance for love even when they're *Lost in the Mist of Time.*

A Twist of Fate

Arianna memory is lost when she suffers a blow to her head. It's 1814 and she's married to Captain Keldon Buchanan, a man who despises her. The more Arianna learns about her life, the more she realizes why she's chosen to forget it. Keldon doesn't trust his wife, but he finds his heart softening to the woman his wife has become. If he didn't know better, he'd swear he's married to another woman and he's fallen in love with her.

Creighton Manor

Zachary Creighton, a gambler with one goal: to win back Creighton Manor. Marriage is not part of the plan, but since he is found with Gillian in his room, reputations are at stake, his included. To keep peace with his reluctant bride, he makes a bargain with her. He needs a tutor for his nephew Tyler, and she needs a roof over her head until they can annul their sham of a marriage. However, Zachary finds himself falling for Gillian's oddly charming ways despite the fact the woman claims to be from the future. The gamble is trust, but will the stakes prove too high for Zachery to risk it all and win Gillian's heart?

Storm Riders

Storm Riders must step in and repair the rift before the dimensions collide. Samantha Skelley and Denny Randeli are sent to 1879 Bodie, California, one of the wildest towns of the west. It should have been an easy snatch and rescue, but Ace McTavish is determined to put himself in harm's way. Samantha and Denny are forced to help him with his plans before they take the next storm ride home.

Rock Star Romance

Two Worlds Collided (Contemporary time travel)

Evie Reid, on a whim, agrees to travel back in time to 1997 to change bad boy Bellamy Lovel's path of destruction. She's smart with a college degree, but she's still fan-girl crazy for the rock band, *Civilized Heathens*. Evie knows despite all Bellamy's smiles and enthusiasm on the stage, he's destined to end it all on one lonely night in a hotel room unless she can change his path.

Bellamy isn't keen on having Evie as his personal assistant, hired by his band mates to watch over him, and keep him on schedule. However, there is something about the woman that sparks his interest, despite his best to ignore her. When darkness threatens to consume him, he realizes she may be the only light that will chase the shadows away.

End of the Road (Ghost story)

Lars Gunner, the frontman for Silent Plaids, died 23 years ago and his death was ruled an unfortunate accident. Despite the fact he can't recall what happened to him in his last moments of life, he is convinced he was murdered. He has been trapped in limbo until his daughter, Cecilia, unearths his journal and is able to see him. She seeks help from

Kaleb, a psychic, but as they resurrect the past, the secrets and lies surrounding Lars' rock and roll life just may be the death of them too.

Heart and Soul
(Contemporary/Reincarnation/ Ghosts)

80s rock star, Haley Rose and her boyfriend went missing without a trace on October 31, 1988 and were eventually presumed dead. Three decades later, thirty-year-old, Rowan Beckett, recalls things only Haley Rose would know, and she can belt out songs in the same unique fashion. However, Rowan couldn't be the missing rock star since Haley would now be in her fifties. Could Haley Rose have come back reincarnated as Rowan Beckett? Or is Rowan as delusional as her family suspects?

Otherworldly Tales...

The Gryphon and His Thief
Some Treasures are Priceless...
A long time ago, a Gryphon shifter's duty was to guard and protect the people of the tribes, but Darrien Andros failed to keep his human wife safe from harm. Cursed for the crime, he must guard everything in the Museum of Cursed Antiquities forever, never to truly live and never to die. Centuries have passed, but when he encounters a thief, who uncannily resembles his dead wife, he is

convinced he has a second chance.

Calli Angelis is hired to steal Hecate's Stone from the Museum, believing she would be returning it to its rightful owner. She never really trusted the person who hired her and now Darrien makes her doubt her motives, too. He also has her questioning the possibility of reincarnation when the attraction between them ignites into something she can no longer ignore.

As the two work together to unravel the mysteries behind the stone, it becomes apparent an old and dangerous enemy from Darrien's past is determined to have history repeat itself.

Magic of the Loch
Michaela and Alan vow to take what time has to offer, but another threat loomed. A sinister shape shifter with a vendetta against Alan is making Loch Ness his personal hunting ground. Now he's threatening Michaela. Alan must discover who the shifter is and stop him before it's too late.

Twilight's Eternal Embrace
If Bram cannot find a way for Adryanna to survive the blooding ritual, their romance is doomed. They seek help from Sheerin, Bram's cousin, who believes he's found a way for the Lathe Sith to survive, but others in the Oiche Sith clan do not wish for them to succeed.

Love's Eternal Embrace (Short story Medieval Ireland)

A knight... A lady... And a deadly dark secret...

A fiend dwells in the forest and Sir Liam Cantwell sets out to slay it. Only the fiend is a fair maiden named Glamis Drui. Will Liam fall prey to her deadly embrace or will his knightly charms be her undoing?

(Vampire legend in the heart of Ireland)

Stake and Dust (Stake and Dust series, Book 1)

Derek Hayes and his family are preternatural hunters. *Stake and dust* is their motto, but Derek has a difficult time accepting his sworn duty when Sloane McBride, his ex-girlfriend from high school, is the one he's been sent to eliminate. Once infected from a Nosferatu bite, there is no turning back. Sloane has been bitten and she will eventually change.

It proves a race against time when Derek puts aside his core beliefs and teams up with Sloane. The Nosferatu wants Sloane for his own, Derek's brothers are hunting her, and every second brings Sloane closer to changing into the very fiend they want to kill.

(Graystone and Hayes tale)

Flowers and Fangs (Stake and Dust Series, Book 2)

Derek Hayes and his family are preternatural hunters. *Stake and dust* is their motto, but Derek has a difficult time accepting his sworn duty when Sloane McBride, his ex-girlfriend from high school, is the one he's been sent to eliminate. Once infected from a Nosferatu bite, there is no turning back. Sloane has been bitten and she will eventually change.

It proves a race against time when Derek puts aside his core beliefs and teams up with Sloane. The Nosferatu wants Sloane for his own bloody Valentine, Derek's brothers are hunting her, and every second brings Sloane closer to changing into the very fiend they want to kill.

(Graystone and Hayes tale)

Abraham's UN-DEAD (Short story featuring the Graystones from Twilight's Eternal Embrace and the Cantwells from Love's Eternal Embrace)

Adryanna and Bram Graystone encounter the Cantwells, another vampyre couple, who question their motives when their actions spark a legend about angels and miracles. It all began when they saved Abraham, a young lad, who would later become the author of the UN-DEAD.

Soul Taker

A vampire, a werewolf, and a Necromancer are a most unlikely team, but Garran, Harrison, and

Isabella plan on putting a kink in the *dubbed* Soul Taker's plans. It's personal now. One of their friends has fallen victim to the Soul Taker's charms, but to stop him from hurting anyone else, their efforts may involve raising the *dead.*

Fallen Angels

Eli: Warriors for the Light (Fallen Angels, Book 1)

Hashasheen demons, assassins for hire, are sent to take out Eli and Ryden. Eli is a warrior and will fight to keep Ryden safe, but time may be his biggest enemy. The Elders gave him until the end of Ol' Hallow's Eve. Ryden must fall in love with him by then or his life will be forfeited.

Lucca (Warriors for the Light, Book 2)
Lucca Marlowe is half human, half angel, one of the Nephilim. Banished for crimes against one of his fellow brethren, the elders bind his glamour and wings, casting him to the human's realm.

Angels and demons demand he do their bidding. His estrange father resurfaces after centuries of being absent and he's brought a friend from Hell. To make his life more complicated, he fears he found his soul mate in a human female. Only Juliet Romeo has a secret that will bring the wrath of Heaven down upon their heads.

It's a race against time to find out who will end up with his soul.

Rodeo Blues (Contemporary Western)

Eight Seconds to Lose the Girl... One chance to win her back.

Tye Casper, a.k.a. the Ghost Rider and champion bull rider, should be the happiest cowboy alive, but when he left home ten years ago to make it big, he said goodbye to the only woman he has ever loved. He's had his eight seconds of glory, but without Jolie Lockhart by his side, the wins mean nothing.

He's been given an opportunity to return home to Skeeter Blue for one last rodeo. He believes fate has sent him there and he'll have a second chance with Jolie, but nothing goes as planned. He soon realizes staying seated on a bull for eight seconds may prove much simpler than winning Jolie's heart.

Wanted (Historical Western Romance)

Sheriff Jace Kelly's wife died birthing his remarkable daughter, Emma. She inherited the families' seer abilities. At six years old, she can't tell the difference between a vision and an ordinary dream. So Jace doesn't put much faith in Emma's recent premonition: marriage for him and a new mother for her.

When JoBeth Riley arrives, Emma is convinced she's the woman in her dream: dark hair, green eyes, and shamrocks in her pocket. There's one problem – she's the notorious outlaw, Baby Face

Jo. Her stay in town is meant to keep Shane Maverick, the leader of the outlaw gang, from finding her before the authorities devise a plan to capture him.

JoBeth finds the Kellys a strange lot. A little girl, who believes her dreams are tales of the future and the rugged sheriff whose kindness proves a distraction. She's an outlaw, for heaven's sake, but Jace is bound and determined to steal her heart.

Fake Marriage with a Dash of Desire is featured in Hot Western Nights (Historical Western Romance- short story)

Jewel ran away from home, not wanting to marry a man twice her age. Nash stands to lose his inheritance if he does not find a bride in three months when he turns thirty. Both are at the mercy of their families, but the two concoct a plan that just might work.

A fake marriage. Later, a quick annulment. What could go wrong? Blame it on the hot summer nights, or toe-curling kisses, but pretending to be married isn't as easy as it sounds.

Made   in   USA   2010

ISBN 978-0-578-05931-0